VERDANT INFERNO

SWITCH
KS-001

VERDANT INFERNO

Alberto Rangel
Preface by Euclides da Cunha

Translated by Thomas Murphy
with Maya B. Kronic

Gonzalo:

> *All torment, trouble, wonder, and amazement*
> *Inhabits here...*

Shakespeare, *The Tempest*

Act V, scene VIII

KS-001

Published in 2023 by
URBANOMIC MEDIA LTD,
THE OLD LEMONADE FACTORY,
WINDSOR QUARRY,
FALMOUTH TR11 3EX,
UNITED KINGDOM

Translated from the third revised edition of
Inferno Verde: Scenas e Scenarios do Amazonas
(Tours: Typographia E. Arrault & Co, 1920)
English language edition © Urbanomic Media Ltd.
All rights reserved

Obra publicada com o apoio da Fundação Biblioteca Nacional e do
Instituto Guimarães Rosa do Ministério das Relações Exteriores do Brasil

Published with the support of the National Library Foundation and the
Guimarães Rosa Institute of the Brazilian Ministry of Foreign Affairs

Copy editor: Amy Ireland

Cover Image; Max Ernst, *La Joie de Vivre*, 1936
© ADAGP, Paris and DACS, London 2021

BRITISH LIBRARY CATALOGUING-IN-PUBLICATION DATA

A full catalogue record of this book is available
from the British Library

ISBN 978-1-915103-08-6

Distributed by The MIT Press, Cambridge, Massachusetts
and London, England

Type by Norm, Zurich
Printed and bound in the UK by
Short Run Press

Contents

Preface
Euclides da Cunha

What we know of Amazonia, even of its physical existence, remains fragmentary. After more than a century of dogged research, which has yielded an invaluable body of literature comprising numerous monographs, it has still only been parcelled out from countless different points of view. Confronted with the most problematic of physical geographies, the human mind has inevitably adopted an *analytic* approach in response. Indeed, this is the only method capable of yielding the requisite elements for a subsequent synthesis. Yet it renders any view of the whole impossible. Even within the narrow niches of the various specialisms, further distinctions continue to proliferate. In fact, this is unavoidable. Geologists, at first wrongfooted by the illusion of structural uniformity, have not yet had enough time to establish a unified palaeontological horizon for Amazonia. Similarly, the combined lifetimes of a great many botanists, from Martius[1] to Jacques Huber,[2] have not been enough to alight upon all the potential specimens to be found in the shade of its palms.... We read their works; we are educated; we are edified.

TRANSLATOR'S NOTES (see also the Glossary at the end of this volume)

1. Carl Friedrich Philipp von Martius (1794–1868), German plant biologist and explorer.

2. Jacques Huber (1867–1914), Swiss-Brazilian botanist, one of the first to systematically study the plant life of the Amazon.

We welcome their finely detailed teachings on the infinite, highly distinctive faces of this land and yet, as we become more capable of distinguishing them from one another, our view of its general physiognomy becomes increasingly hazy. We are left with a great many sharp and vivid outlines, but they are for the most part highly disjointed. This enormity which we can only measure and partition eludes us; it exists on such a scale that it must be broken down in order to be evaluated; its magnitude can only be perceived once it has been enlarged using microscopes; it is an infinity to be administered in tiny doses, gradually, slowly, indefinitely, tortuously.

Yet it is worth reminding ourselves that this overly analytical, long-winded discourse was quite inevitable from the outset. For human intelligence cannot be expected to suddenly become capable of bearing the weight of such a portentous reality. It must grow alongside it and shape itself around it in order to master it. Take the example of Walter Bates:[3] this great naturalist spent more than a decade in Amazonia, making momentous discoveries which lent support to the then nascent doctrine of evolutionism, but during this period of hard labour he never left the narrow coastal strip between Belém and Tefé. From there he astonished the institutes of Europe; he won the admiration of Darwin; he rewrote, or rearranged, many chapters of the natural sciences. Yet at the end of such a fruitful enterprise, he could still be quite certain that he had not exhausted even the limited patch of space in which he had taken up residence. He had not seen Amazonia. And because of that, he saw more of it than his predecessors had.

This is only natural. This land is still mysterious. Its space is like Milton's space: it hides within itself. It is cancelled out by its own vastness, extinguishing itself, collapsing on all sides, bound to the geometric destiny of the planet's curvature, and fooling all enquiring eyes with the deceptive uniformity of its immutable aspects. To truly *see* it, one must renounce any intent to *unveil* it. One must reduce

---

3. Walter Bates (1825–1892), English naturalist and explorer who accompanied Alfred Wallace on his great expedition to the Amazon in 1848.

it, subdivide it, narrow it down and, by the same token, further specialise the various fields of study just as Bates did, as did Frederick Hartt[4] after him—just as today there are the naturalists working at the Museum in Pará.[5] Today they embark upon a project which no doubt will yield such a protracted series of partial conquests that it will make the last three centuries' work seem like mere reconnaissance.

This is a thousand-year campaign against the unknown. Victory will only be won in the far-distant future, on the back of untold labour, as the final veils are torn away from this marvellous place which today renders our eyes dazzled and vacant.

But by then Nature will have given up all of its secrets. The definition of every last feature of Amazonia will mark the conclusion of Natural History as such....

*

Let us imagine, however, a heroic intellect, one who dares, recklessly, to contemplate this Sphinx all in one fell swoop.

In the face of this vertiginous, dazzling wonder, he is bound to falter. This book is proof of it.

Nervy and rebellious lines, scribbled out in defiance of all humdrum formulae, reveal to us in graphic detail manifold trails, twists and turns, crossroads that hurtle off in every direction, looping back from all sides, zig-zagging, happening upon detours, shortcuts and abrupt dead ends; sometimes in a rush of impetuous advances, sometimes in sudden impromptu retreats, here wrongfooted by the most alarming paradoxes, there following the straight and steady practical

---

4. Charles Frederick Hartt (1840–1878), Canadian-American geologist, palaeontologist and naturalist who accompanied Louis Agassiz on the Thayer Expedition to Brazil in 1865, and thereafter specialised in the geology, flora and fauna of Brazil.

5. The Museu Paraense Emílio Goeldi in Belém in the state of Pará, a research institute and museum founded in 1866.

insights of a soul wandering among splendours, utterly intrepid and completely lost.

Verdant Inferno, beginning with its title, could not have been anything other than what it is: startling, original, extravagant. It is sure to occasion the surprise, distaste, and instinctive antagonism of mainstream criticism, which is a criticism without any jagged edges, a sleek and audacious translation of the higher aspects of human culture into a banal conception of art.

For this is a barbarous book, barbarous in the classical sense of the word: it comes from elsewhere. For this very reason, although it is built up out of nothing but truths, what they yield is a collection of phantasies. A painful realism pulses through each and every page, yet it seems to be engineered by a particularly fiery brand of idealism. Alberto Rangel is apparently every inch the poet, albeit one too exuberant for the discipline of metre or rhyme, but at the same time he is an engineer, addicted to the coldest and most calculated of technical processes. The startling reality of Amazonia entered his eyes through the lens of a theodolite. Fantastic scenes played out for him inside perfectly triangulated grids. He staggered on like a daydreamer, but one guided by a compass at all times. His wild poems were scratched out in the back pages of his surveyor's notebooks.

Rangel has unwittingly inverted certain extremely vulgar preconceptions surrounding artistic creation. What we have here instead is a temperament as seen through the lens of a new vision of Nature. He did not alter this. He copied it, traced it. Hence the surprise it is bound to occasion. The urban critic who does not understand this book will be its best critic. For what is fantastic and incomprehensible is not the author, but Amazonia itself....

His receptive art attempts to encompass the whole of this land and to amaze us with its marvellous abundance of life. It will surely astonish us. A pantheism this extreme is something we cannot hope to comprehend.

The writer alarms us with the simplest of natural descriptions. What is customarily known as 'still life' stirs powerfully beneath his pen; galvanic flows seem to irrigate these lines in which matter is no longer passive, and objective things seem to take on anomalous personalities.

Forests that wander slowly, travelling across the plains, cautiously scaling steep ravines, the stupendous, immobile clamour of a perpetual and formidable struggle in the disorder of their twisted branches. Lakes that are born, grow, join together and swell as their tumultuous existence unfolds, and then recede, wither, decay, perish, die out and rot away like extraordinary organisms subject to the laws of a monstrous physiology. Rivers that roam the waterlogged solitudes like cautious hikers, fearful of the inconsistent terrain, proceeding 'with the cautious disposition of the antennae that form the furos'.[6] These make up a reality hitherto unseen, emerging in the chiaroscuro of the unknown in the guise of an incorrigible idealism....

A scholar would unveil all of this to us by leading us down the endless, cushioned steps of cautious analysis, taking care not to startle us. The artist achieves it in a single leap; he sees it; he contemplates it as if from above; he tears the veil away in a single gesture; he lays bare its majestic purity.

In truth, the Amazon is the last page of Genesis, yet to be written.

Its instability is the result of accelerated structural formation. A metaphysician might detect in it a singular carelessness on the part of nature, which, having carefully constructed the infinite modalities of natural phenomena everywhere, had started to rush at the last moment and completed its job haphazardly, hastily correcting a slip-up at a spot that it had passed over by mistake. Natural evolution caught in the act.

While elsewhere it is dwarfed by the vicissitudes of the evolutionary transformations of the earth, and must extend itself outward in time in order to relive, in retrospective prophecies, the thousand-year-extinct lives of fossils, here the panorama of human life embraces whole cycles of dramatic orogenic transmutation. The dynamics of

---

6. Networks of channels which pass through undergrowth, connecting together major rivers, igarapés (smaller watercourses) and bodies of water. Notably, they can be traversed by canoe.

geology cannot be deduced, they must be seen; and geological history is still being written every day before the delighted eyes of those who know how to read it. Hence the surprises. We are so keen to see the balance of natural forms everywhere that some have appealed to the confused hypothesis of catastrophism to explain subtle changes; in Amazonia, extraordinary visible transformations result from the simple play of the most common physical forces. This is a young land, a land still in its infancy, a land in the making, a land that is still growing....

It quickens, vibrates, and gasps, tumultuous and wild. Its telluric energies hasten to obey the universal tendency toward equilibrium. Its physiognomy shifts before the very eyes of the stationary spectator. In such inconstant landscapes one imagines the whims of mysterious wills at work.

Even from a drily topographical point of view, there is no fixing it into definite lines. Every six months, the flood acts like a wet sponge on a half-finished sketch, erasing, modifying, or transforming even the most salient and apparently solid outlines—as if the restless brush of an irrepressible superhuman artist were sweeping across the canvas of its boundless plane....

*

Then, caught amid the magic of these vivid scenes, a tormented protagonist appears: the human. Rangel's whole book is concerned with the contrast between the two.

And so the plot thickens. The writer's attitude is brought out in sharp relief. The anomalous fantasist aspect of his character only becomes more prominent as, line by line, we see it forced to adjust itself to the terrifying appearances of reality.

Yet we excuse him; we applaud him. In this beautiful, bold gesture, Alberto Rangel captured a critical, fleeting moment in time, one which history will never see repeated.

This joy serves as compensation for the rebarbative nature of the subjects he treats.

In the Amazon of today, this cruel antilogy is playing itself out: on this abundant land, which continues to grow in the joyous fullness of its existence, a dying society is in wretched turmoil....

We need not describe it here. We have this book, which encapsulates and commemorates the signs of this suffering. Better than anything we could achieve using grandiose concepts, it poignantly captures the scenes of a deplorable collective agony, across eleven chapters which are like eleven Rembrandt miniatures, redolent with terrifying symbolism.

Looking at them, you will see ebb and flow, among the wandering folk of this land which denies them their very physical stability, slipping away from them into 'fallen land' and flood, the yearnings and prodigiously high hopes that they labour for and keep alive through their sacrifice.

'Maibi' presents us with the image of an Amazon mutilated by the myriad blows of the rubber tappers' homicidal hatchets. In 'Hospitality', a fallen man returns to humanity for a few seconds by some miracle of atavism, before plunging once and for all into the shadows, thicker by the day, of his irremediable moral decrepitude.

In 'The Tenacity of Life' we are shown a monstrous community— its organs not yet fully developed, at once newborn and dying, suspended in a vegetative state by some miracle of nature whose gifts it has monopolised to the detriment of more robust races—a community which in other territories would succumb, weakened, crushed by natural antagonisms.

In the other tales we find the same pessimistic and grim quality. This is quite understandable.

At times upon this extraordinary land, the simplest of physical elements and the most serious of moral systems come together to express the same fateful event. Take 'Obstinacy', for example.

The tragedy unfolds without a moment's hesitation, and with an immediate, fulminating outcome. A potentate covets the land of an unprotected caboclo.[7] He takes it from him, with the collusion

---

7. *Caboclo:* a person of mixed indigenous Brazilian and European ancestry.

of a corrupt judicial system. Yet the caboclo is stubborn and seeks to overcome this tremendous injustice with a mad gesture: in order to remain on his land for all time, he buries himself alive, and dies there. It is simple, it is far-fetched; but it illustrates a certain feature of the social structure of the Amazon. In his frenzy, the savage grey reproduces the unconscious struggle for life he has seen in the lower biological orders.

Man kills man just as the parasite annihilates the tree. Humboldt's enchanting Hylaea[8] has this terrifying lesson to impart:

> The apuizeiro is an octopus in plant form. It wraps itself around its sacrifice, extending thousands of tentacles over it. Gilliat's octopus had eight arms and four hundred suckers; those of the apuizeiro are uncountable. In the structure of its tissue, every one of its microscopic cells takes the form of a thirsty mouth. And the whole struggle takes place silently, without a whisper. It begins by curling around the branch, which is attacked by woody threads, coming from who knows where. Then these threads swell, and, once swollen, begin to proliferate into others still. Finally, the weft thickens and advances slowly, in order to mesh together with its prey, which it completely replaces. The apuizeiro is like a shroud enwrapping a corpse: the corpse rots but the shroud lives on, immortal.
>
> The abiu tree would have only a short time left to live. A desperate effort could be sensed in the miserable creature, determined as it was to break free from the noose in which it was held. Yet its captor seemed to become stronger, gripping this unfortunate organism that was being strangled by the gradual, unexpected pressure with each and every one of its constricting fibres. The process was irreversible. With a machete, the tentacles could

---

8. 'Hylaea' is the term Alexander von Humboldt used to describe the South American rainforest. It is from the Greek for 'wooded area', Ὑλαίη, and derives from Herodotus. See A. von Humboldt, *Views of Nature*, tr. M.W. Person, eds. S.T. Jackson and L.D. Walls (Chicago: University of Chicago Press, 2014), 47.

be torn to shreds and ripped out. But it would be enough if just a small piece of capillary filament was left stuck to the tree. This would allow the executioner to reattach itself to its victim, who would have no chance of survival. The polyp is part of a colony of polyps. Generations live in a single body, in a single part, in a single fragment. Every part, no matter how small, is alive. It cannot be reduced to an individual. It is the solidarity of the infinitesimal, essential, elemental, inseparable and indivisible in the republic of synergetic embryos. What remains is always enough to bring it back to life. It reproduces easily, in its latent but irrepressible haste to procreate more and more.

The abiu tree's canopy of small leathery and glabrous leaves had almost disappeared into the broad foliage of the monstrous parasite.

In fact, this duel between forms of plant life represented a perfectly human spectacle. Roberto, the potentate, was himself a social apuizeiro.

A botanist would certainly describe the malignant *Moraceae* in greater detail, beginning with a serious enquiry as to its genus (*ficus fagifolia*?... *ficus pertusa*?...) but could never hope to paint its striking features so vividly. On the other hand, a sociologist would struggle to find any concept to equal the synthetic eloquence of that final admirable image.

*

The above extract is typical of the style of Rangel's book.

It is easy enough to recognise: choppy, agitated, restless and impatient. It is not relaxed, stretched out across the amplitude of the sound waves of the word, allowing quiet thoughts to expand as they will. It constricts itself between the staves, fading into unexpected punctuations, pausing in moments of sudden reticence....

In acoustic interference, points of silence are explained by the interaction of sounds which cancel each other out. And there is a kind of mental interference in these brief, often inconclusive, fleeting moments, under the constant blows of an overabundance of ideas. One feels that the writer is among men and things, some of them dubious, barely emerging into view, appearing for the first time, shrouded in mystery. His thoughts are either volatile or incomplete, suddenly diffusing into the vagueness of hesitation so as not to deviate too much from the positive truths that are being revealed to him. Descriptions give way to images. Indeed, it would be impossible to subordinate to fixed rules—which result from long-term cultural processes—the impressions aroused in us by a land and a people which has barely arrived at its own distinguishable identity, one which is only just visible through the initial glimmers of civilisation. And besides, Rangel himself was astonished at these scenes and settings and, in an outpouring of sincerity, refused to repress his astonishment or to rectify, with the mechanical coldness of the professional writer, his vertigo and the mutiny of his exasperated sorrow.

He was quite right to do so; it made for a great book.

Within its pages you will find certain flaws. However, one must distinguish between those of the writer and those of the subject.

For who, having penetrated so deeply into the darkest core of our primitive and coarse nature, could resurface without being covered in the muck of the abyss?

Moreover, our critical faculty is itself unstable, its current verdicts transitory. Before exercising it upon works of this kind, whose anomalous appearance derives from their profound originality, we should remind ourselves of the false and inauthentic aspects of the mental structure of we Brazilians, in which reactants alien to the genius of our people have come to predominate. We think too much in French, in German, or even in Portuguese. Almost a century after political autonomy was won, we still live in a spiritual colony. From the construction of sentences to the sequencing of ideas, we pay excessive respect to the precepts of exotic cultures which dazzle us, and we bow to peculiar received, *a priori* states of consciousness, blind to the real conditions of our life, so that our own personality disappears, besieged by new attributes that truncate or soften it, or blunt its original edges.

Here, what we see as a writer is not a spirit that draws strength from the stimulating suggestions of the objective materials that surround it, but an intelligence that denatures itself through a systematic dissimulation. A sort of physical mimicry is established by way of this cowardice which leads us to align ourselves, through external resemblance, to those peoples that intimidate and enchant us. So that, even when it comes to our own things, we cannot resist obeying the prejudice that we should be as un-Brazilian as possible. We translate our texts with great erudition into European Portuguese, forgetting that we ought to take the greatest pride in the fact that the Portuguese would find it difficult to translate or even to read our language.

In any case, it is time to emancipate ourselves from all this.

It is quite right that, in the case of the sciences, whose superior philosophical reflections seek to establish the universal solidarity and harmony of the human spirit, we should bow to all foreign influences.

But no master from beyond our borders shall guide our artistic impressions, or even pretend to interpret them. The impeccable phrasing of Renan,[9] who sculpted the convulsive face of the Gnostic, could not depict the cauchero[10] for us; the lapidary concision of Herculano[11] would seem inexpressive in the majestic disorder of the Amazon.

For the new scenes and the new dramas before us, then, a new style, although, for all its inevitable daring, we do not consider it flawless.

That style is what this book uncovers.

Besides which, it is ennobled by a splendid sincerity.

Here is a great voice, hovering, impassioned and avenging, over the florescent hell of the rubber trees, which the opulent jungles garland and insidiously tint with the illusory colours of hope.

Euclides da Cunha

---

9. Ernst Renan (1823–1892), French orientalist and polymath.

10. Cauchero: a worker on a rubber plantation.

11. Alexandre Herculano (1810–1877), historian, novelist, and poet, a figure of considerable national prestige in Portugal; one of the first romantic authors in Portuguese.

1. The Tapará

...and the lands of the Amazon are full of such lakes...

Father João Daniel, *Treasure Discovered in the Upper Reaches of the Amazon River*

This remote shore of the Tapará, seen from the other side of the river, is a dark braided cord that borders a wider band of lighter cloth. This cord is woven of wispy, sad willows like eyelashes surrounding an immense dilated but blind pupil. Behind this frontline of riverside vegetation, as if wary of being overwhelmed by the water of the Amazon, are the more cheerful embaúbas,[1] tall with silver-backed leaves and white trunks which give the impression of having been enfeebled by parasitic aphids, fungi and lichens.

After them comes the forest, which looks like it has come to a halt because they were blocking its path. It appears as a mass of mountain-green, a colour that remains constant all the way up into the heights where it curdles into shapeless and sparse canopies. All of it is the same: a packed, disorderly clutter of branches and foliage, twisted fronds, tangled up with balls of liana vine that cling to the boughs. It seems to be struggling against itself, at once conflicted and at peace.

The sun takes advantage of a fork in the branches or a retracted twig to shine its fiery light through the interstices of the mass of greenery. Sometimes it passes through in fine threads, sometimes in daggers. These daggers embed themselves in the trunks, while the

---

1. The trumpet tree: a fast-growing, short-lived tree used for medicinal purposes, which grows along riverbanks (*Cecropia peltata*).

threads are made of the most tenuous, volatile gold filaments, making the leaves into pieces of jewellery studded with enamel baubles. There are sections where you might think candelabras had been lit for an elven feast. The light, however, never manages to flood into the forest, but can only sneak through the gaps, spilling out and spreading. It is soon contained, because in the end everything has the impenetrable consistency of a vast conglomerate of porphyry.

The bank these willows adorn is a beautiful and harmonious curve of the lip, but every track ends in a muddy embankment. There, the caboclo's canoe bobs and steadies itself in time with the banzeiro, the series of waves sent out by the passing transatlantic liner.

From this beach on rotting land, soft as a sagging mattress, it is difficult for the fisherman to enter the forest by going over the ridge, which passes through where the igarapé[2] was during the floods. Just days ago, they were still paddling through that forest. It was a more straightforward affair then: just sink the laurel paddle into the water and float along gently. No load on the shoulders, no sloping ground strewn with crags and depressions.

When it has been submerged by a flood, the forest suits the native better. In the Amazon floodplains, humans would do well to exchange their lungs for gills. Everything is accessible to those in the water. The remote interior harbours no secrets when the gangliform network of lakes connects up with the arterial network of streams. The caboclo is free to wander, as safe as someone travelling on well-mapped roads, and goes wherever his quiet intuition tells him the easy catch is to be found. For him alone there is no mystery to this hinterland.

But then, when the flood comes to an end, man is stranded, or, even worse, trapped. As the water recedes, so does his ability to wander. He can no longer float along, and is like one of those logs that floats up to the surface only finally to be weighed down by the water, sinking to the bottom of the river to rot. Although this is not always the case: sometimes it may form the first stake in a structure which will come to be decorated by utricularias, pístias, and pontederias and

---

2. Term for a canoe channel in the Amazon.

mortared in by mud, and will later become an island, altering previously charted maps and changing the known routes.

The trail through the forest is hard to make out. Even if it lasts until the end of the flood, there is no time for it to become well-defined. What can still be seen here and there amid the tangle of branches, where the heaviest flood marks the trunks, are branches that have been severed by blows from an oar after getting tangled in the bow of a canoe and then pushed aside. Besides, there would be no point in tracing the route any further; it would always be like a line made in chalk, rubbed away by the flood acting like a kind of sponge.

It is a long way. A mere two and a half kilometres, but it seems endless. The use of the canoe, of course, which confines one's feet, leads to irrepressible fatigue and impatience. The ground is regular in level and of an unchanging alluvial nature, but littered with fallen trees, tangled with stalks and branches, dead or in the lethargy of drought, awaiting their inevitable revival with the flood. Hanging here and there in dry clumps of vegetable matter, hard and dark pendants, the cauixi,[3] a flower with the texture of a burlap sack, blooms, shedding an imperceptible pollen. It is this pollen that invisibly causes a caustic burning sensation on the nape of the passer-by's neck; unless it is the poisonous bullet ant or taplú wasp with its red-hot sting....

In the dry October the first rains have not yet fallen, which means that the beginning of this Amazonian deluge, which will last longer than the one in the Bible, is a month away. The forest burns. There are no crackling flames, nor the wavering blur of fires; it burns without any light at all. The fire is something one feels, a type of spontaneous combustion. It comes above all from the astounding fermentation process that the vegetation undergoes in the moisture trapped beneath the taller branches. And all of this takes place in an agonising, oppressive silence.

At midday, the forest is eerily silent; at night, it is astir in a Wagnerian chorus composed of voices ranging from the insane clamour

---

3. A freshwater sponge which forms clumps in the roots of trees by the riverside in the Amazon (*Metania reticulata*).

of souls wandering in a fit of despair and pain to the faint whisper of a single rabeca[4] in the most delicate *smorzando*.

The heatwave anaesthetises the monstrous organism; the nocturnal dews cause it to suffer bad dreams and night terrors. One would think that the moon, regulator of the planet's oceans, was stirring the equatorial forest into terrible high tides, like a sea of foliage, even more conducive to shipwrecks....

There is a moment when a certain brightness breaks through the gloom of the forest. A skylight opens up amid the breus[5] and sparse lacres,[6] and a trail of light makes its way along the ridge of the ravine, precisely following the scarp, made steeper still by the to-ing and fro-ing of pacas[7] and agoutis.[8]

The forest too, as it were, stands on the edge of an enormous narrow valley cradling a wild rice field which has the soft colour and fullness of new alfalfa. And in this pale green blanket, to the right, there shines a round plate of polished steel. This lowland is the lake, the Front Lake, the name of which announces the existence of the Tapará further along the valley. The shining steel plate is made up of the remainder of the water that did not manage to escape, forced by the difference in level to remain there as a watering hole and a refuge for herons, ananís, carões, arapapás and wild ducks. Imprisoned water. Enraged at this situation, a hate-filled gaze, as of a basilisk, seems to seep through the sclera of the lake. The pool takes its revenge, breeding a surfeit of low life: algae and poisonous microbes. Whoever drinks from it will later have to settle accounts with their spleen and liver. A hydrographic curiosity, this dry lake is an alchemical laboratory of malarial microfauna and microflora. And it is so quiet down in

---

4. A type of fiddle originating from Portugal.

5. A south American evergreen species (*Protium heptaphyllum*).

6. A medicinal shrub that grows in tropical climates (*Vismia guianensis*).

7. A large rodent found in the Amazon rainforest. The name is from the tupi *paka*.

8. Another native rodent, a relative of the guinea pig.

the pit that no one would ever know. Only mercury at the bottom of a vat could be so tranquil and mirror-like.

To reach the Tapará, you must cross the lowland where that immobile retina, embedded in the orbit of the ravines, stares at the sun with a spasmodic and unnerving persistence.

Still bogged down in the soft mud of the headland, there is another ravine to cross, which raises up to form the outer slope of a fortified parapet on the opposite side. You must climb over it, first guessing where the interrupted path re-joins the long basin of the empty lake. The search is not easy. The sprawling branches of the identical trees and the lacework of the araçaranas[9] conceal its location. You just have to guess! At last the trail emerges, with the distinctive appearance of a very faded line on an old route to a mysterious mine. Well-accentuated at first, it is then lost, just like the other one, in coils and squiggles through the forest. It is a fantastical route: one that has been borrowed and run along by a watercourse. The markers had already been set up; it was just a matter of picking them out of those that had been laid out and collimating them, keeping an eye on the rays of sun on the canopies....[10]

The poorly marked path continues across the spine of an imperceptibly higher sandbank. Perrault's Hop-o'-My-Thumb[11] would need to drop pebbles along such a path to mark the way.

---

9 A shrub native to Brazil which produces a fruit variously known as Amazonian pear, Brazilian guava, or strawberry guava (*Myrcianthes gigantea*). The name *araçarana* in Old Tupi means 'araça-like tree' (*rana* 'similar to, like'), suggesting a passing similarity to the araça (*Eugenia stipata*).

10. A reference to the collimation method of calculating difference in elevation, a surveying technique Rangel would have been quite familiar with. Since it involved the use of a theodolite and lens, it would have been important not to be surprised by an errant sunbeam.

11. A reference to one of the fairy tales published by Charles Perrault: *Le petit Poucet* rescues his siblings from the forest by leaving a trail of stones.

Suddenly, once the curtain of abiuranas[12] and acapuranas[13] has been drawn back, a new border of araçápixunas[14] dominates the landscape, in a broader, deeper and more water-filled lowland: the Tapará. The immense lake twists to one side and the other, as though a giant were pushing the undergrowth aside and digging deep into the earth with its fingernails until hitting water. This valley comes as a surprise. When traversing the forest, it seems so dense that you'll never be able to get rid of its thick, rough, green gum. There are no clearings. The heavy vegetation, on level ground, with no cliffs or terraces, will continue like this all the way south to the vague plains bordering Mato Grosso and Bolivia, creating the disheartening impression that there are no gaps in this density whatsoever. The lake therefore stands out—a clearing, a respite. In the infinite continuity of the tunnel, this vent through which the light enters is significant; it offers relief from the feeling of having been buried alive. It reminds us that, up above the constant view of vaulted walls and shadows, the sky is still there.

There are large puddles along the shallow channel, sifted clean by the gentle tapestry of grasses. With the light bursting into the hollow of the trench, the lively fauna resemble an engraving representing a piece of land in the last part of the first chapter of Genesis, scratched out by the naive burin of an old engraver.

Around these pools assemble innumerable wading birds and waterfowl. Their young are still barely feathered. And in the slimy, soggy lair a whole bustle of flapping wings and various calls can be heard.

Flights attempted or made, the thrashing and squawking of the Tapará's feathered population does its best to impart an unexpected

---

12. Name for the *Pouteria* genus of flowering trees. The name comes from Old Tupi *abiu* 'fruit with tip' and *rana*, 'similar to, like'.

13. A tree with pink flowers and high-quality wood, with various well-regarded medicinal properties (*Campisiandra laurifolia*). The name is from Old Tupi acapu (*aka*, 'top' and *pu* 'tall') meaning 'tall top', 'tall tree', and the suffix *-rana*, 'like', as above.

14. Arazá, a fruit tree native to the Amazon rainforest. Araçápixunas are a dark red, tart, but flavoursome variety (*Eugenia stipitata*).

liveliness to this forgotten site of industrial exploitation, despised by geographers and not exactly overrun by surveyors.

Under the crushing tendrils of the branches, what this magnificent lake offers, even with the squawking and the fluttering of the birds, is a deadly desert environment. Everything is bare stone, and even reptiles would flee from the heat reflected from those slabs. This lake resembles the Dead Sea, despite the greenery of the banks and the exposed bed, carpeted with grass and populated with a paradisiacal fauna. The classical image of Charon also comes to mind, as if, to cross such stagnant water, that funereal skipper had to wield the jacumã[15] of his igarité[16] of Death. This is what the Acheron must have been like, encircling the depths of Hell—just like this furrow of dead and infected water bordering a dark, ecstatic jungle. Perhaps it even recalls that lake where Heine placed his languishing countess[17] to drift among the spectral faces of the amorous and drowned.

Although the banks of the Tapará are enlivened by the soaring pomp of white and brightly-coloured feathers and the cawing of birds, life is certainly more intense at its watery core—a life of skins, scales, and shells. Alligators sleep placidly on the mudflats, alongside crafty fish and timid chelonians.[18]

When the river withdrew, sucked up by the summer, it left behind it a slime composed of thallophytes.[19] It also left behind a whole ichthyological catalogue drowned between the shores. And because the

---

15. From the Old Tupi: a type of oar that also serves as a rudder. Charon is making use of the local equipment.

16. A type of traditional canoe with a canopy covering half of it.

17. A reference to Heinrich Heine's poem 'Countess Jutta [*Pfalzgräfin Jutta*]', in which the titular countess is being rowed over the Rhein and is reminded of the potential suitors whom she had ordered drowned in order that they would not break their oaths.

18. Belonging or pertaining to the reptilian order *Testudines* (formerly *Chelonia*), comprising turtles, tortoises, and terrapins.

19. The division of the plant kingdom that includes lichens, algae, bacteria, and slime moulds.

liquid diminishes further each day in November, these fish continue to pile up. Then something hideous takes place: the lake starts to rot.

The reptiles seem to prefer the swampland. They snooze with their snouts in the mud, looking for all the world like black rocks rolled from the fringes of some ravine to the quagmire of the plain. The shells of turtles intermingle with the dark, raised backs of muddy fish....

All the horror of that lake is then manifest. There is no more staring at the golden light, nor at the greenery of the vegetation that frames it; there is no distraction. The lake seems to stifle the joy out of all creation. Slimey, putrid, and mephitic, it can send the observer's consciousness into a state of madness. To believe that someone could live in this place and harbour hopes of gaining fortune or comfort from this rottenness is to launch one's reason into a vertigo of insanity.

No, this rotten quagmire can only be a just punishment for the curiosity of ambitious explorers. Perhaps some cruel deity safeguarding the virtue of the Amazonian hinterland offers this prize to violators of the land: to come across the most repulsive and profound manifestation of the corruption of life, spread over the surface of just a few hectares.

The promised Valley of Josaphat is to be a place of resurrection, yet it will certainly be less moving than this ghastly pit, full of mud, pus and the palpitations of life, all mixed together.

Here, in one place, it would appear that the essential struggle, which Bichat[20] understood in his incomplete notion of life as the reaction against death, is present in large proportions, but death is overwhelmingly victorious. Even the broncos alligators that bask luxuriantly on the sprawling marshland end up victims of this lethal bed, lending their bulk to the general decay. What enters into the dark recesses of their throats is a broth of bacterial cultures, which is like honeycomb to them. Yet its ferment makes them burst at the seams, in spite of their monstrous armour. Their banqueting table is the coffin in which they are laid to rest....

---

20. Xavier Bichat (1771–1802), French anatomist and pathologist, author of *Physiological Researches upon Life and Death* (1800).

In this narrow basin there is an abundance of unfortunate creatures that did not make it into the shoals which, returning to the waters of the Amazon, managed to avoid the prison that now incarcerates those who were late or too careless. They are happily left to their fate of being putrefied, either individually or in groups. It takes one or grabs the whole pack. Then the heat and humidity combine in the tragic interplay of merciless forces that constitute this dreadful process of decomposition.

But on the edge of this abyss of decay, high above the plain, are two miriti[21] huts.

Old Palheta and his son do their salting there. In September they moved from the *terra firma* to the straw salting houses on the lake, bringing their wives and dogs. These poor creatures stay for four eternal months, perched on the edge of that pit....

However, they are unimpressed by the catafalque set up in the waterhole; this lake has been familiar and friendly to them since they were children. They even want to get the legal title for the land they occupy. A stamped seal of paper guarantees you six feet under....[22] It grieves them to know, vaguely, that Chico Mendes, as part of a comprehensive campaign involving the use of powerful weapons, intends to take over the miserable huts in which they have settled.

Next to the two ramshackle dwellings, valuable pirarucu hides are stretched out on the horizontal poles of a tent, testifying to the fact that some prudent activity is taking place in the midst of this graveyard.

While it is still at the entrance to the lake, right next to the upper mouth of the Autaz the water flows in an abundant stream. Leaving this funereal basin, they use a humble cedar or laurel montaria[23] which delivers them to the world, just as, in the opposite direction, it delivers them to solitude and labour.

---

21. The Miriti are a traditional riverine people of the Amazon who raise livestock and gather natural resources including the miriti fruit (*Mauritia flexuosa*).

22. In Brazilian Portuguese the phrase is 'sete palmos de terra': seven palm-widths of earth. Both phrases refer to the traditional depth a body needs to be buried at in order to prevent malign odours from rising to the surface.

23. Montaria: a small canoe, made from a hollowed-out trunk.

Soon, however, this mode of transport is exhausted until the next flood; the mouth is a mere tear duct and the men are stuck at the shore of the lake. But they do not rely on it. There is neither discouragement nor despair. They come voluntarily to the wilderness to repeat this struggle year upon year—the same edition, the very same print run of a book. They stay one step ahead of death, but only just, by travelling to the necropolis and snatching from it whatever they also want to kill.

All of their business, which they manage together and which is largely limited to parsimonious exchanges in the taverns on the coast, is based on and guaranteed by the work of salting on the lake.

Providence is at work here: without the amazing accident of these hydrographic formations, so finely tuned and so regular, the caboclo would not be able to survive half as long. And in this incredible collection of congenial tendencies, the lake is the best feature. Whether during drought with the jatica,[24] or in the flood with the arrow or harpoon, although by no means abundant, it is a truly precious resource.

Faced with the invasion of the battalions (of cosmological and moral forces) that weigh down upon him, the Amazonian takes refuge in the lake. It satisfies the stomach and the imagination; in the first case, because it is his 'larder', as he likes to call it; and in the second, because the lake is a beloved site of legends, a secluded theatre of mysterious dangers.... Here it pleases the Mother of the Waters[25] to emerge, and here the Cobra Grande[26] also makes its home, making

---

24. Also *jateca*. A long-stemmed harpoon, used for turtle fishing. From Tupi *atyká*.

25. Also known as Iara, a figure from Tupi-Guaraní mythology resembling a nymph, mermaid or siren. The name comes from Old Tupi *y*, 'water', and *îara*, 'lady': thus 'lady of the waters'. Many manifestations of the myth have the Iara leading men to a watery grave through seduction. In Mário de Andrade's classic of *modernismo*, *Macunaíma* (tr. K. Dodson [London: Fitzcarraldo, 2023]), the eponymous hero is famously tricked by an enemy into an amorous encounter with an Iara, who proceeds to tear him apart and steal his muiraquitã amulet.

26. Also known as the Boiúna or 'black snake', the Cobra Grande is one of the most well-known mythological creatures in the Amazon. As the name suggests, it is a gigantic snake, often endowed with the ability to assume different forms,

terrifying noises, along with packs of caatinga-scented jananaíras,[27] rabid and ready to attack.... In the forest that engulfs him, curupiras,[28] caiporas,[29] matitaperês,[30] and boitatás[31] pass by in a sarabande of panic and terror.

The rubber catastrophe has yet to descend upon Lake Tapará and many other places. In countless areas, barriguda and seringaranas trees[32] serve as a reminder that industrial exploitation is impossible. Since they are not suitable for firewood, nor is their milk elastic, yet

---

such as canoes, in order to trick fisherman to their deaths. On dark nights, its eyes are said to look like two lighthouses floating in the water.

27. In indigenous mythology these packs of forest dogs would intoxicate their victims with the scent of caatinga (forest vegetation) before devouring them.

28. A humanoid mythological creature covered in red hair, with its feet turned backwards. The footprints it leaves behind therefore have the effect of confusing hunters, who will pursue them in the wrong direction. Their name comes from Old Tupi *kuru'pir*, 'covered in blisters'.

29. From Old Tupi *caapora*, meaning 'inhabitant of the forest'. The term was also used to refer to escaped slaves living in the forest.

30. Specifically, a striped cuckoo, the *Tapera naevia*. In this instance it refers to the legend of the saci, a one-legged Black man who smokes a pipe and wears a magical red cap. In some versions of the myth, he is able to transform himself into a matitaperê at will. His cap famously smells appalling.

31. From Old Tupi *mba'etatá*, literally 'fire thing'. Because of the similarity between the Tupi word for snake, *mboîa* and thing, *mba'e*, the term was later thought to be *mboîtatá* (literally 'fire snake'), thus giving rise to the myth of a fire serpent in modern Brazilian folklore. The mytheme appears in the letters of Joseph of Anchieta, in a passage which also mentions the curupira (see above). This is presumably one of the earliest occasions these names were written down: 'There are also others [...] who live by the sea, or along the rivers, and who are called baîtatá, that is, things of fire [...]. They appear at night in a bright flame [...] attacking and killing the Indians, like the corupira....' Padre José de Anchieta, *Cartas ineditas* (São Paolo: Instituto Historico e Geographico de São Paulo, 1900), 48.

32. The former, *Heavea microphylla,* is a variety of rubber tree that only produces very low quality rubber. Its named means 'potbellied', because it responds to its flood habitat by producing a swollen or bellied trunk. The latter, *Sapium marmieri*, does produce latex, but was supplanted in importance by the more commercially successful *Hevea brasiliensis*.

they look just like a legitimate rubber tree, they are seen as a mockery of the real thing—a vegetal parody. A simple incision in the cortex of their huge trunks causes apparently priceless sap to flow out in an abundant stream, but this white blood does not coagulate upon being smoked: the liquid is merely sticky or brittle, but not elastic. Instead of being priceless, it is a disappointment.

The caboclo will reflect that it is better this way, perhaps. For otherwise, the wave of immigrants, the Cearense,[33] as he would put it, lumping them all in together under a generic term that carries a vague hint of spite and contempt, would rain down like a plague, invading the forest.... They would exterminate all the game and fish, ambitiously and unscrupulously taking over the land in which he had been born. That people who arrived yesterday are already taking such delight in a victory that the old native still aspires to and cannot achieve!

Little does the caboclo suspect that, in the enthusiasm of the new society encamped in the Amazon, he, with his reserved character, with a certain sadness at being exiled within his own homeland, comes to serve as a happy and unshakable moderator.

For when the tapuio[34] or mameluco[35] people, fishermen, become embroiled in the battle of a lifetime, their resistance will not be a brake on the rubber tapping mania, but it will limit the conflict; a conflict that is quite natural given the tremendous interplay of the ambitions

---

33. People from the northeastern state of Ceará, who were subject to a large internal migration process prompted by drought, which Euclides da Cunha describes in *Amazon*, 33, 38. The *Grande Seca* of 1877–1878 led to over 100,000 Cearense migrating to the Amazon. These waves of internal migration were in particular made up of *sertanejos*: inhabitants of the *sertão*, the semi-arid hinterlands made famous by the novels and short stories of João Guimarães Rosa. Of the ways in which these Cearense immigrants were taken advantage of upon their arrival, da Cunha wrote: 'The emigrant *sertanejo* has created an anomaly here that cannot be overemphasised: he is the man who toils in order to enslave himself.' E. da Cunha, *Amazon: A Land Without a History*, tr. R. Sousa (Oxford: Oxford University Press, 2006), 38.

34. Word for an indigenous Brazilian who has become assimilated or accustomed to the culture of the coloniser.

35. The child of a European man and indigenous woman.

of the outsiders, which with their little axes, their little bowls, their buckets and boiãos,[36] have turned the whole land over, shaking it down for electricity and steam, the evils of those societies that see themselves as powerful and sophisticated.

These tendencies, one passive and almost indifferent, the other often destructive and immoral, are located in the Lower Amazon, whose inertia restrains the Upper Amazon. In the Lower Amazon, restricting the thirst for force, is this lake which dampens the fever of the rivers, the fever that makes the pulse of Commerce beat harder, but in the end damages and corrupts one of the most defamed and bountiful corners of the planet.

The lake is therefore worthy of a chapter by Michelet.[37] It also deserves the cool eye of a sociologist; both a hymn and an analysis....

The lake itself is a sanctuary. It does not matter that beyond its shores there might be some nobody who does not want the needy to get their due, whether because the fish are scarce in the rivers, or because they have been swindled out of their money.

So enormous is his struggle that, in this lake amphitheatre of the Amazon, the caboclo is the Orestes of Greek tragedy, pursued by furies. Yet the wretched man makes his strongholds in these hidden lakes where the surplus water, coming down from the tributaries or falling from the sky, is swallowed up by the Lower Amazon; a place where he could only be extirpated by a lengthy siege (and perhaps not even then).

This 'extirpation', however, is just a manner of speaking. Nothing is lost.... The blood that will one day flow through the veins of the average ethnic Brazilian, the blood of the pariah tapuio, will have the plasma of so many peoples as part of its molecular composition, mortared into a single body, fired in a single crucible, cast in a single mould. Crucible, mould, body: apparatus and residue of a consummate

---

36. In this context, the term for a type of clay chimney used for the commercial production of black rubber.

37. Jules Michelet (1798–1874), French historian best known for his gigantic *History of France*.

transformation in which, what with the mameluco, the carafuz,[38] the mulatto and the predominant Indo-European immigrant, the Brazilian will have become the definitive type of ethnological equilibrium. In the end, it will no longer be what it has been: an enfeebled medium for the transfusive traffic of races....

---

38. Of African descent.

2. Catolé's Concept

But whatsoe'er he had of love reposed
  On that beloved daughter; she had been
The only thing which kept his heart unclosed
  Amidst the savage deeds he had done and seen;
A lonely pure affection unopposed:
  There wanted but the loss of this to wean
His feelings from all milk of human kindness,
And turn him like the Cyclops mad with blindness.

Byron, *Don Juan*, Canto III

In the main room of the Administration house, the old Administrator, adjusting his spectacles and leaning over his large registration book, was interrogating a bumpkin who stood before him with the use of coarse language and harsh slurs.

In the room, roofed by bare tiles without a lining, there were only two windows overlooking the paddock, where it seemed there had once been a vegetable patch and a garden. There was still some cabbage and an Arabian jasmine plant growing in the otherwise bare beds.

'Have you already chosen your plot, you good-for-nothing?' asked the official, his quill aloft, throwing a bespectacled glance at the settler.

The latter stammered, 'Yes Sir, the sixty-fourth, next to Miss Martinha, on the other side of the Passarinho.'

'Not that one!' started the Administrator. 'I already have someone down. I might have known you were trying to get Mundico's lot...'.

The bureaucrat had indecorously reserved the best slice of land for his brat of a son.

'But I didn't even...'

'No dirty tricks here. Nice try, but I know your sort, lowlife.'

'In that case, the fifty-seventh...', murmured the newcomer timidly.

'All right then!' And the head of the Colony entered the chosen number in the registry.

Then, closing the bulky book with its metal corners and leather cover, he calmly ordered the new recipient to leave, rebuking him, 'You'd better take care of the lot, you papaya sucker![1] I don't want you to be a deadbeat, do you hear? The Government is filling the bellies of these good-for-nothing devils!' he grumbled.

João Catolé had arrived in the Amazon on the loading ramp in Fortaleza along with the cattle. He had come with his little daughter, fleeing the miseries of the sertão, where not a drop of water had fallen and where his beloved wife had perished. He had barely been able to look away from the dead woman when, one day, he came across her body sprawled in the shade of a carnauba tree. The poor thing had come from the waterhole. Jesus Christ, her clothes were stained with red, like a murderer; and, because she had brought her hands to her mouth, trying to hold back the haemorrhagic vomiting, her hands were also drenched in blood.

It was while they were praying The Agony in the Garden at the feet of the dead woman that the woebegone João made up his mind to leave Santa Quitéria. It did not take much to sell a few calves and some bushels of flour, get to Maranguape, and take the railway to the capital. He got on a slow ship and hopped off at Manaus without a cent to his name. He was all skin and bones. His first and only shelter was in the basement of the Sá sawmill.

From São Raimundo to Educandos, on the city's bustling banks there stand modern houses with their sparkling glasswork, entablatures, and platbands, and rising high above them, the peaks of the Matriz and Remédios towers and the dome of the theatre. Under the haematosis of progress, a prodigious transformation of the shacks of the old town of Barra do Rio Negro into the Amazonian metropolis of today has taken place. Quay walls, wharfs, tall house fronts, the market building and its 'ramp' form the frontline of the city, running alongside the black ribbon of water, which bathes it funereally.

---

1. Mamão-macho: An insulting term for people with long, thin faces.

Next to the market, on land built up by alluvial deposition but which the swelling river still continues to flood, there is an immense warehouse made of old planks. In anticipation of the flooding, it was built on a high, poorly-set stilts, and the water leaves it completely untouched.

All day long this immense building throbs with the gurgling of the boiler and the sound of saws tearing up logs, slicing cedar trunks into beams and boards. At night the upper part is silent; below, between the slimy rotten piles, people live, for a few months at a time, a dismal nocturnal life. This filthy hiding-place is home to many miserable souls who disembark from the 'birdcages'[2] or the larger passenger ships from the south in order to seek sustenance, and perhaps even riches, in the enchanted land of rubber.

A gypsy camp, where families settle in squalor in the understory of the tenement workshop.

An incomprehensible building, which remains stubbornly on display as a mockery of the civilisation that surrounds it, the sawmill is a kind of friendly asylum. This free hostel has no sign and charges nothing for accommodating the needy and the unfortunate. A heart beats in its bare, rigid chest of beams and rafters. In its shabby humility, it takes pity on the destitute who seek it out. There are no wardens and yet the most perfect order reigns. An ideal society, egalitarian in nature and apparently disciplined by the common dream of making a fortune, the dream that has brought them all into the same underground den where they settle in comfortably and unceremoniously, absorbed in the daily routine of setting up hammocks, heating pots, washing and rinsing clothes....

The bosses or their intermediaries turn up to find people to work up above. Pack wolves on the prowl around the equatorial izba.[3]

---

2. 'Gaiolas', literally 'birdcages', are paddle-wheeled steam riverboats. Tradition has it that they are so-called because of the sparse comfort afforded to passengers, who sleep in hammocks on the exposed decks, lending the vessel their distinctive appearance.

3. A type of Russian wooden cottage (an extension of the image of the wolves which chimes with the construction of the warehouse).

Promises are made, glittering like mirages, and contracts are soon signed or scrapped. Fate and Business make the rounds of the besieged camp....

One day a group leaves the banks of the river; the next day another group arrives to replace them, taking up residence in the ruined pavilion.

João and his daughter were among the residents of the hideous hostel of this colossal tijupá.[4] However, the Ceará native specifically resisted the temptation of the rubber tree. The main obstacle to his fascination with it came from thinking about his little daughter. Imagine taking the girl up there with him! You couldn't lose, they said, but those type of people say many things.... Women were sold, young girls were snatched away from families, no one knew how, and his Malvina would soon be a woman. No! He would stay in Manaus, near Flores, where they said there was a government colony. If he went there he would have land, and even food and medicine!

Determined to get himself established in that little spot, he inquired about the route and set off, having armed himself with a letter from the Diretor de Terras.

As soon as the head of the Colony had finished assigning him his plot, Catolé began to settle in, carrying his small leather suitcase to the house. This tract of land was one of the few that had such a building, although it was barely covered; capoeira[5] had grown over it and it had been abandoned while still new.

Catolé had chosen the plot after having spent two days exploring the colony, which he had scoured in every direction. The plots were divided up into large areas covered in thick undergrowth and lined by numerous small watercourses that resembled tremulous calcite veins in limestone. The area was bisected by the main road, wide and carriageable, which sloped down from Cariri to the campos geraes of Rio Branco. A few plantations had emerged in the dense undergrowth of laurel and acariquaras,[6] centred on little mud houses covered in

---

4. From the Tupi: a shelter built in the forest.

5. A term for the tough bush that grows back on ploughed or burnt land.

6. An evergreen tree historically used in construction (*Minquartia guyanensis*).

Marseilles tiles. There were a few pineapple, manioc, cashew, and sugar cane plantations, as well one or two rice paddies in the lowlands.

The colony had made no progress; it was like an exotic arctic plant withering in the heat of a greenhouse. The occupants were not interested in ploughing. They preferred to track down agoutis, pacas, or capoeiro, shooting them on the central footpaths and selling the game in Flores or at the city market.

The administration's efforts to build bridges and houses, to provide medicines, ranches, machinery and schools, met with apathy from the locals, who were always complaining and dissatisfied. First and foremost, they blamed the land: it was no good, it was degraded, sandy, useless clay...there were ants everywhere.... With the despondency of exiles on a rock, the settlers spent their days forlorn among futile lamentations.

Only João blessed his luck. In Ceará he had never been able to own a piece of land. He had always been a day labourer, either on rented or borrowed land. He could maybe have owned a stretch of carrasco[7] or some cave on the high slope of the mountain where the pumas live, but what was the future in that?

It was the Amazon, that cursed land of rubber and malaria, that made him a property owner; when the migrant from Ceará arrived, it gave him land, food, a roof over his head, medical assistance, education.... The life-devouring monster at the foot of the heveas was, in fact, also a protector and friend.

In high spirits, he shored up the hut that had been given to him, cleared out the weeds, and after just a year he had four quadros[8] of lush, clean plots that made his allotment stand out. Later, Catolé managed to install a 'flour house'[9] in the porch, with all the essentials—

---

7. A kind of dwarf forest composed of shrubs with slender stems and branches; a form of vegetation that is more scattered, ragged and rough than caatinga and that is largely composed of *Senegalia monacantha*.

8. A Cearense term for a parcel of agricultural land comprising a square that is 75 metres by 75 metres.

9. A place for the preparation of manioc flour.

the wheel, the stool with the 'caititu' grater, the press, the oven, and the winnowing basket.

Three years had passed since the guest at the sawmill had become a settler. But it seemed like only yesterday that he and his little daughter had decided to come and work in the colony.

Malvina was about thirteen years old at the time. She helped him out a great deal. The young girl even joined her father weeding and harvesting. She put a wide straw hat on her head and took out one of his pitchforks; she was a man! Catolé would often stare and wonder: the oval face, the blue-green eyes and the laughter were those of his deceased wife, but she was more resolute and hard-working. The girl did not have a minute to herself. She took care of the house, the laundry, the kitchen, the livestock, worked in the sieve fields, and still had time left over for lacework. How beautiful Malvina was with the cushion on her lap and the bobbins jumping up and down in her nimble hands, making the sound of castanets shaking feverishly in a samba! The catolé wood the bobbins were made from clicked madly, but the thread was wisely woven between the pins in the pricking pattern.

João had only a few acquaintances in the colony. The most frequent visitor was his neighbour Rosália, who one sad day had come to tell him that her husband had been crushed by the umarirana tree which he had been felling. She had run to the field, screaming like a madwoman, where she found the man with a wide hole in his skull, out of which the soft, whitish mass of his brain was oozing. When the old woman arrived he was still warm, but already quite dead. Some other settlers came to help. The next day, the delirious woman tried to stop them from taking the corpse away, kissing it as though it were the effigy of a saint. They shooed her away with pity. In the hammock, crossed over with a stick, the limp body went on its way to Tarumã,[10] jolting around in the cart, the widow's desperate cries resounding in the distance.

Rosália was inconsolable. When she came to Catolé's house, her favourite subject was always her memories of her husband.

---

10. Location of the municipal cemetery in Manaus.

Malvina would tenderly keep her company in her longing for the past, and the old woman would sigh, as if relieved for a moment of the pain that would not let her be.

Apart from Rosália, Pedro Carapina was a regular visitor. The story of this Ceará citizen was in the same general vein of all those who have emigrated. On the outskirts of Canindé he had been struck by the tragic horrors of the endemic drought. A thirst had gripped him. Thirst, but also ambition. He had arrived as a boy: bored by the monotonous routine of the vaqueiros,[11] he could not resist the urge for adventure, and had stripped off his leather jacket and leggings and set out. In fact, he had been even more compelled by the example of a cousin, who, having been presumed dead, had returned from Acre, where he had worked under the orders of Plácido de Castro 'killing Bolivians', with plenty of clothes, a parasol with a silver knob, a watch, a hefty chain, and a pile of money that he frittered away instead of roasting in the caatingas and fields of the sertão.

Pedro worked in the sugar mill which the administration had set up at the Colony's headquarters, and spent his Sundays and holidays drinking coffee with his friend João.

João had no suspicions as to the frequent and repeated visits of his countryman.

But Malvina could scarcely conceal her joy, drawn as she was toward the carpenter by a feeling that she was powerless to resist. When Pedro arrived late on one of his usual days, Malvina became restless, unable to control herself. Finally old Rosália received her confession: that her growing love was preoccupying her and filling her with happiness. The confidential exchange between the two women was full of dreams and longing.

One day, the brazen Administrator made João a proposal: he wanted to employ João's daughter as a light labourer in the administration house. He would give her a good salary and fair treatment....

---

11. Cowboys from Ceará, who round up cattle in vaquejadas (also a sport involving rounding up a bull on horseback, which exists to this day).

The loving father had been loath to part with her. But in the end he had consented; it would be a way to increase the resources that were so scarce; and it would even be advantageous for his daughter to learn the refined habits of the whites. She would learn something, welcomed into the casa grande to consort with 'knowledgeable, city folk'....

He reflected on the matter repeatedly, and finally ended up handing the young girl over to the Administrator's family.

The girl was on her best behaviour. Everyone praised her gentle manners and her tireless dedication to her work.

Pedro continued to work at the sawmill. The labour was neverending. The Administrator complained every day, uttering the harsh and abusive expressions with which he fertilised his zeal as a state employee.

'Well? Mr Pedro Malasartes, will you or won't you finish making this bloody trough? Huh? Save your false expression for the Most Holy. I've had enough already!'

But the work dragged on and on, as if he were stuck in this stupid rut forever. Pedro did not even put more effort into his work when he was threatened with being replaced. He spent his days setting up a moulding, constantly stopping to sit in the corner of the yard, distracted, smoking a cigarette....

From there he could see Malvina at work, coming and going in the yard or through the house. Immersed in contemplation of her, the hours flew by, one cigarette followed another, and the endless work at the mill acquired the status of the martyrdom of St. Engrácia.

One night, the Colony was shaken out of its usual sleepiness by an astonishing event.

Rifle shots had been heard outside the administration building. It was not long before the whole story was known. There had been a terrible drama involving bloodshed in the darkness. During the night Pedro had abruptly injured another employee, killed the Colony Adjutant, and dragged poor Malvina away with him, no one knew where.

Descending so suddenly upon that sleepy enclosure of scrubland and meagre crops, this tremendous event shook everyone.

'But why?' 'How did it happen?' 'How horrible!' 'What about the girl?' Questions and exclamations rang through the agitated Colony.

In a flash, the news reached the ears of João, who, in the throes of madness, weeping unrestrainedly, plunged into the haunted forest, on the trail of the fantastical pair, lost in the vortex of foliage.

The silk of the sky was embroidered with the gold pink of the dawn by the time they found Catolé supine, looking like a dead man. His feet were full of tucumãí thorns.

They lifted his body and brought him into the house. He awoke from his unconsciousness exhausted and delirious. 'My daughter!... Malvina!' he cried out. And his cries seemed to move even the heavy woodland around him.

And for many days, while emissaries, settlers, and soldiers searched the surroundings in every direction, from the Tarumã waterfall to the Grande igarapé, from the Rio Branco road to the west, the thought of those two miserable wretches oppressed everyone.

Finally, they grew tired of searching every nook and cranny of the underbrush and finding nothing. The fugitives were clearly far away by now, safe from Justice, carried forth by the strange passion that had impelled them.

A week later, half a hundred crows, flapping above a certain point in the forest, kindled dark forebodings. Some of the settlers took off to the spot above which the sinister flock of scavengers was hovering. There they found the corpses of Pedro and Malvina lying side by side, their skeletons falling apart in the midst of a nauseating gruel. A rifle lay on the ground among the filthy remains.

Authorities from the city confirmed the details of the tragic affair and drew up the appropriate papers, burying the mysterious pair of wretches right there. In a discreet and unforgiving malachite vault, the forest was left to guard the secret of that scene, the madness of those creatures, the romance of the crime, and the rotting bodies.

For a long time after this, the whole colony suffered from an indefinable malaise. An air of ruination lay about everything. The forest itself seemed despondent; when the wind blew through its melancholy greenish-yellow fronds, it reminded one of the wails of mourners.

Little by little, an indolent calm returned to the colony. Things and people slowly returned to their former torpor and the quiet, indifferent life they used to have. João Catolé remained in his corner like a humble animal in a burrow licking a wound that would not stop bleeding. He was a grieving shadow, living in squalor and despondency. Never again did the field see him with hoe or pitchfork in hand. Some life did remain in his eyes, enough to give them a bruised and haunted look, as if focused on something inside himself, a terrible memory that could only be dispelled by countless tears. A post in the hut had broken. He had not fixed it. Termites thrived in the slats and stilts. What did he care? Unpleasant vines crawled across the roof and wild grasses spread everywhere. He was in such despair, he had neither the strength nor the courage....

'Malvina! Malvina!': João would wake up at night, calling for his daughter. In his dreams he saw dreadful forests; making his way violently through the trees and thickets, he would furiously chase two fleeing shadows. It was a terrifying race as they collided with one another here and there, injuring themselves on spines, getting bogged down in swamps. The two shadows were always getting further away.... He awoke with a sore body and a heavy sweat on his rough, cold forehead.

One June morning the cold set in, causing the miserable Catolé's weak limbs to curl up and shiver. The pitiful man went to sit outside, in the yard, on a rotten carana[12] trunk, to bask in the bright sun like a lizard.

Just then, a settler passed by on his way back from hunting, a pica-pau rifle[13] slung over his shoulder. Peeping out from the small bag he carried were the reddish heads of two cotiara cobras. The hunter touched his hat in greeting and stopped.

'So, Mr. João, how are you?' Without waiting for an answer, he looked out over the abandoned field, where the passion-fruit blossoms had bloody sores, and went on. 'This land is the devil...nothing grows here.

---

12. A flowering palm (*Mauritia carana*).

13. Literally 'woodpecker': an old muzzle-loading rifle.

Only cashews and pineapples. In Ceará it's different, there are vegetables...it's because of the winter.[14] It's not even worth it here....'

And in a deep sigh, João replied loudly, opening up in a brief, scathing speech: 'What, the land? No, the land's fine! It's man who is no good.' Bowing his head melancholically, sighing and stricken, João Catolé fell back into the sad state of perpetual banishment. He remained silent. He was invaded by a wave of tenderness for his daughter, rotting in the forest, and in that tenderness bloomed a feeling of justice. The madness of that infamous patrician murderer who had wiped out her happiness had afforded him the clarity of this verdict....

When history comes to analyse the development of the Amazon, along with the rest of the world, it might do well to adopt the unfortunate Catolé's synthetic concept as an epigraph.

---

14. Sharecroppers in the sertão were highly dependent on the winter rains to provide water for their crops and animals.

3. Fallen Land

Your courage you must summon up,
Your love, your blood, and god of human will.

Alfred de Musset, 'Suzon', *Premières Poésies*
(tr. Marie Agathe Clarke)

José Cordulo's house on the bank of the river stood out owing to the presence of an old and solitary mongubeira, perched high up in the ravine. This tree stubbornly repeated the habit of bursting into large pink flowers every year, followed by enormous crimson fruits. This strange tree, without any leaves whatsoever, would have dangling from its arms these great lacquer urns which, when they ripened and opened up, would shed onto the ground soft pieces of gossamer fleece.

On this piece of wasteland, the caboclo raised a small herd of cattle in five quadros of field planted with mium and colonia grasses.

In summer, these xerimbabo[1] helped themselves to the muri[2] in the low water, but they became pitifully thin, their wasting away aggravated by the ticks upon which the ani birds[3] fed. One or two didn't make it. Summer, like a plague, was claiming its victims. The small pasture was thin, low, and yellowed by the sun, as if it had been carefully trimmed

---

1. Old Tupi for 'very dear thing': a domesticated wild animal, a practice well-established amongst the Tupinambá.

2. A type of aquatic grass.

3. A type of bird belonging to the genus *Crotophaga* in the cuckoo family. The name is probably from Tupi, although this has not been established, and was first used in Georg Marcgrave's *Historia Naturalis Brasiliae*.

down using scissors. Often, they had to resort to using a field in the lowlands, borrowed for a while from a richer neighbour.

Beyond the dying field, which had assumed a strong sepia hue, around the hut an enormous clearing was outlined in the rough strokes of coarse charcoal. Cordulo had set fire to the field, but it did not burn well, so he had to hoe it all down. The esplanade was therefore cluttered with trees semi-carbonised by the flames. Branches stood upright, giant trunks lay scorched, victims lying in wait as if still ready to repel anyone who tried to attack them. The bristling of the prostrate stems was like a war song, cutting through the disorder of the ranks when the hour is late and all is despair in the raging turmoil. They sang a hymn to victory, standing in the middle of the scorched blackness: a taperebazeiro tree[4] shrouded in its upturned fronds, with twisted branches, and some caiaués,[5] inajás,[6] and tucumãs,[7] their spatulate palms licked by flame.

After the October rains, however, the rest of the summer, in November, would give them time to burn the remaining coivaras.[8] Everything would be cleared. And December would see the pale green stalks of corn pointing out across the ferocious but temporarily subdued land.

José Cordulo had earned a reputation as an indefatigable worker. 'Caboclo jaguar!', he was called by the Cearense people in the area, who admired the extent of the caboclo's crop fields.

It had been more than six years since he had married Rosa, a skinny yellow woman from Rio Grande do Norte, whom the ship from the South had brought down with a miserable bunch of immigrants who were travelling to the Colony. She had come with her father, an old

---

4. A deciduous tree which produces a yellow fruit (*Spondias mombin*).

5. The American oil palm (*Elaeis oleifera*).

6. The maripa palm. Produces a yellow edible fruit. (*Attalea maripa*.)

7. Another type of palm. Its fruit is sometimes used for making wine. Its seeds are used to make tucum rings, which are worn by Christians in Brazil. (*Astrocaryum aculeatum*.)

8. A specialist term used in this slash-and-burn farming method: a heap of twigs or sticks which the fire has not completely burnt, and which are gathered to be reduced to ash.

man who was barely able to stand on his legs, suffering from myelitis and asthmas, and who was satisfied to see the plot that had been distributed to him by the Director, eat the Government's grub for a few days, and finally be buried in a grave among the guava trees of the São José cemetery.

Still, the caboclo loved the Cearense woman. He had left a nomadic life on the water because of her and decided to work on the land. By raising cattle using the 'take half and leave half'[9] strategy, planting corn, beans, and manioc and rearing some chickens, there was always enough to support them. Four children, two of whom the girl had given birth to at the same time, were his greatest source of joy and strength of spirit. The curumins,[10] whom he doted on with a smile, would jump at his neck, accompany him to the fields, and he would bring them ingá pods,[11] tinamou eggs, whatever he could find in the forest....

Even if all the cattle were infected, pestilence ate up the entire field, or the fruit trees became diseased, Cordulo would still be happy....

Always with his machete in hand, from sunrise to sunset, he would not let go of his work. The only time he took a break was for hunting, fishing, bundling up tobacco, or sealing the canoe.... He only rarely strayed from cultivation and raising livestock, namely when he was obliged to by the ajuri,[12] or to serve as a godfather in Itacoatiara, or to help out in some emergency—for the land, which was so fertile, could also be harmful....

In a few months, even before the corn's cobs began to form and the beans to blossom, the field would end up packed with bindweed and São Caetano melons. The jurubebas, taxizeiros, embaúbas, and taquaris would then arrive, undoing all of his hacking and burning,

---

9. A rule of thumb for grazing management where, to keep the pasture healthy, you allow the animals to consume one half of the plot while the other half re-grows.

10. Nheengatu for 'kid, child'

11. A fruit with a sweet-tasting pulp, also known as ice-cream beans (*Inga edulis*).

12. Tupi word referring to the communal assistance given by smallholding farm-ers at planting or harvesting time, also known as muxirão or mutirão.

prompting a great deal more cursing and hard work. To stop them it would be necessary to keep active with the spade and the machete. If Cordulo closed his eyes for a moment, when he opened them the obstinate forest would have returned to the place from which it had been repelled.

The forest makes a vigilant sentry of the farmer. Leave your post and it will vigorously burst through the lines of the field, taking possession of it again. The difficulty then increases. The forest that returns is swarming with shoots, spikes, vines, and stems. It comes back in the form of capoeira, more densely packed with branches and thin stems and therefore all the more impenetrable.

With the forest, cutting down the undergrowth is easy and the axe is enough to finish off the sweeping destruction initiated during this phase. But the axe is useless when attacking new capoeira, and only the machete will suffice to cut down the thick green covering on the ground. It is an endless task. The vegetation, branchy and small, curls in on itself, fresh and compact. If it is like that in the forest, it is the same in the fields: everything turns back into wilderness. And when the weeds are spreading, the mata-pasto creeping shrubs always come into play, attempting to smother the useful panicum and other grasses. But here fire is still the farmer's best friend. In summer, when the fences and crops are protected by a strip of cleared land, it rages devastatingly until the first rains in October or December. In just a few days, it makes the blackened and hardened land reappear miraculously.

Everywhere, at this time of year, billows of smoke rise into the sky from all points on the horizon. September is the month of sooty, crackling fires. The flames of thousands of blazes tear through the Amazon rainforest. It seems that the delirium of the flame will turn the surrounding plains into a single fiery ocean. Nothing will remain. Not one green canopy of a tree in this sea of fire.... But the forest defends itself with its humidity, and only its edges are charred. The conflagration finally dies out in the very place that had provided its fuel—the deforested clearing.

In front of José Cordulo's house, the orange trees, lined up at the foot of the ravine, were withering, dying of a mildew that had quite literally covered their bark and leaves since last winter. Two coconut trees, under attack by insects, had yellowish palms. One cupuaçu had inexplicably borne no fruit. There were only a few clumps of taiobas[13] and tajás[14] and some bacabeiras[15] and pupunheiras,[16] that plant whose fronds had served as the immense headdresses[17] of savages.

From high up in the yard, you could see upwards to Ponta Grande, Igarapé-Açu, Iranduba, Lake Tapiíra and, even nearer, the spur of the Mauari, a rocky outcrop that the river strives to demolish through the desperate efforts of its boisterous current in all directions; and down to São Pedro, the reddish ravine of Bararuá, obligingly hosting the cawing jacamars sitting around in their nests, and then the soft and prolonged curvature of Santo Antônio below.... On that Saturday afternoon, the smoke from the fires surrounding the city darkened the air, well in advance of the twilight grey. A divine artist was smudging a charcoal sketch of the land. Thus, the borders on the other side of the river, already indistinct because it was far away, became at that peaceful hour even more hazy, smothered in floating bands of black crepe.

It was for the other side of the river that Cordulo would have to leave at dusk, to go to a party with his family, since he had been invited by his friend Pacu.

On that stretch of coast at the moment there was an unusually high volume of montarias, all heading in the direction of the promised party. They were packed with people and luggage, as if it were the departure of some bandeirante[18] expedition group.

---

13. A species of flowering plant in the genus Xanthosoma. It produces an edible corm. (*Xanthosoma sagittifolium*.)

14. Heart of Jesus, a plant with impressive green and red heart-shaped leaves (*Caladium bicolor*).

15. A fruiting palm (*Oenocarpus bacaba*).

16. The peach palm (*Bactris gasipaes*).

17. In Tupi this headdress is called a *canitar*.

18. Bandeirantes were parties of explorers in the early days of Brazil's colonisation who would seek precious resources and capture indigenous peoples as slaves.

As soon as it got dark, a 'birdcage' came down the river, lit up, coruscating, like a strange firefly with lanterns all over its body rather than just its head or abdomen. The caboclo went down to the small port with Rosa and the children.

The bright, round moon was rising, unfurling its shimmering band of flashes and reflections across the river.

With a trunk accommodated at the back of the canoe, over the ribs, and his wife and curumims tucked up under the woven palm canopy, Cordulo, at the bow, pushed away with some force. Rowing calmly, he straightened out into the reach, where the pebbles glittered gold in the soft water.

At that moment another steamer was heading off, also completely lit up. The regulation red and green beacons shone out like a ruby and an emerald among the glittering gems on its huge sparkling hull. Cordulo's montaria parted the waves that the snouts of these glistening Leviathans left in their wake. The pounding of their propellers could be heard as they went along embroidering the profuse and palpitating pattern of the lights onto the water like sequins. A piraíba[19] rose up and, with a formidable splash, plunged its body back into the camlet and filigree of the river.

It took a good two hours to make the oblique crossing in the radiant splendour of this brocade. Announcing the party were the sounds of musical instruments, velvety at this distance, in the water and the night.

Veering close to the canaranas[20] on the bank, Cordulo bumped into a dozen or so montarias tied up in the port. As the beat of a cheerful polka rang out clearly, interrupting the muffled sound of voices and feet tapping on the ground, Pacu's hut appeared, lit up like one of the boats.

---

19. An extremely large catfish (*Brachyplatystoma filamentosum*).

20. German grass. An aquatic or semi-aquatic perennial that proves very productive on the Amazonian floodplain. (*Panicum spectabile*.)

It took some doing for Cordulo to disembark, jumping over the hulls of the other montarias, which were wedged in close and tied to one another.

A path, newly widened, led through the canarana fields to the yard of the house surrounded by cacao and abiu[21] trees. In two rooms, couples were canoodling and dancing. Leaning against the windows, in the quiet, a number of guests looked on. In the puxado, the outbuilding adjoining the house, and under the veranda where many hammocks were set up, there was a bustle. Caboclas, some of whom were elderly, cradled their children or grandchildren, while others, by the expertly constructed fire, prepared cocoa and coffee. People passed into the rooms with China trays covered with cups and glasses. Eggnog, vinho abafado[22] and aguardente were distributed to everyone at short intervals. Caboclinhas, smelling of priprioca[23] and vanilla, moved in chattering groups from the house to the exterior, and from the puxado and veranda back to the rooms inside: 'Axi![24] Tertulina...' '...Manduca didn't come to the dance. He's at the lake, he says, with Cazuza...' 'Comadre[25] Caterina is waiting...' 'Cousin! Come on...'. They adjusted the frills on the bodices of their dresses, or the jasmines tied at the nape of their neck in a neat twist of the hair, all in the same style.

---

21. A fruit tree (*Pouteria caimito*).

22. 'Muffled' wine. A type of wine prepared by caboclos (from ingredients including cashews and genipa) and kept covered for a few days in order to refine its flavours. Not to be confused here with Portuguese *vinho abafado* which involves a short fermentation period for the grapes interrupted by the addition of spirits or other wines.

23. A tall grass found in the Amazon. It is used in cooking and is known for its fragrance. It is the main ingredient in a *banho de cheiro*, a traditional aromatic bath taken on special occasions, which might be what is being referred to here (it also involves vanilla).

24. An expression of irritation or disgust from Pará.

25. The mother of one's godchild.

The cavaquinho,[26] guitars, rabeca[27] and clarinet played restlessly, splicing together various dances. The players took turns with some of those who danced. Untiring, the gentlemen, in their shirtsleeves, embraced the dolled-up ladies.

And so the hours passed quickly for these people, in this intoxicating bustle of partying and revelry, breaking up the monotony of country life on those sad shores.

The morning had broken, gathering a thin mist over its rosy chest, which the sun, like a golden button, closed chastely. High as it was, it looked down upon a party still in full swing. The revelry would perhaps continue until the next day. As long as the curral[28] kept up the supply of turtles and the flour bowls were not yet empty, why end the dance? Cordulo, however, felt tired and unenthusiastic. He remarked to his friends: 'Ah! My time!...' and allowed himself to be carried along in the conversation, glancing over at the frenzied, entangled pairs jumping around in the stifling atmosphere created by the dust scraped off the floor as they dragged their shoes.

Under the cacao trees, groups of hammocks were set up in which some of the more sleep-deprived and languid guests recovered their strength. At the water's edge, others washed their changes of clothes. And so the party went on, merrily stirring up the crowd of caboclos who had even come from as far as Parana da Eva and Conceição do Serudo to enjoy themselves....

No one wanted to leave. During the day, the band had been replaced by a harmonica, but at night, with the same round, white moon spreading its fulgurations across the river, the instruments picked up the jittery thread of the dances once again.

Cordulo was determined, nevertheless, to depart, and while he waited for Rosa and the children to get ready, he calmly smoked a cigarette rolled up in a tauari leaf, taking part in a conversation with

---

26. A small guitar, originally from Portugal.

27. A type of fiddle.

28. A pond where turtles are kept as a food supply, particularly in anticipation of the water receding.

a group of others. Suddenly, everyone in the peaceful surroundings heard a loud crash, like the distant rumbling of thunder.

'Must be fallen land',[29] observed old Pacu. Everyone agreed with their compadre's explanation.

From the yard radiated the penetrating perfume of reseda and cape jasmine, planted among crotons and pepper trees.

Couples were taking part in a contradance by the flickering light of lamps set into niches in the walls, when Cordulo, along with Rosa and the children, got back on the montaria. The compadre's pleas for them not to leave had made Cordulo realise that the next day was Monday. The others, bachelors, could remain; he had 'a plantation to see to and a wife and kids to feed and clothe'.

At the bow, José Cordulo rowed on in a sea of jewels. The banks were the same streak of black paint, but the surface of the river was the chimerical background of Eldorado.... Already far away at this point, the music from the party was dying off into faint gasps. Only a few frayed remnants of the soft sounds pierced the night, through which the moonlight cast its ghostly magic.

This crossing was quite difficult, particularly because the river was restless, fluctuating in the undulations of a strong banzeiro.[30] Arriving near the shore, where his mooring should have been, Cordulo became puzzled. He no longer recognised his land. What had happened? Was he drowsy or demented? He ran the back of his hand over his tired eyes: nothing.... Where was his home? He stared hard at the dark stain of the ravine and could not make out its location. He had not been mistaken; of that he was sure. Tapiíra and Mauari were visible up there...he could clearly distinguish the flagstones of the latter, and down there was old Arcângela's chestnut tree, there was Terra Preta....

When Cordulo brought his montaria closer to the bank, he recognised that he was indeed right in front of his property. But the land had

---

29. Extreme land erosion caused by the Amazon river.

30. An Amazonian term for the agitation in the water caused by passing steamboats or wind in the still waters of rivers or lakes.

collapsed and the whole plot, along with the mongubeira[31] tree, the hut, the corral and the orange trees, had disappeared. Now it was a bare, jagged line on the shore. The piles of burnt branches, which had originally been at the back of the house, now grew out of the barren riverbank, a line of battlements on the crest of the cliff wall. Cordulo had fallen through a trap door, losing five years of incessant labour. It had been so much effort, day by day, hour by hour, only for all the dreams, all the hard work, all of their possessions, to be annihilated by the absurd—the disappearance of the land itself! Even though he had built a future on the most solid of foundations, those foundations themselves had collapsed! Building on the earth had been like building in the clouds....

The caboclo felt an oppression that cut his breath short at the obstacle presented by this 'fallen land'. In the bottom of the canoe, one of the little ones whimpered in Rosa's thin lap.

Paddling solemnly, Cordulo headed straight towards the embankment, searching for a less steep way up the collapsed land. He groped his way up. At the top of the slope, the man was welcomed by the trees from the burn, which lashed him once more. He made no complaint. He preferred heartfelt and productive gestures over empty words.

On the following day, the sun came out. Our victim was triumphant. The caboclo, surrounded by his wife and children, planted the mainstay of his new home in the ground above the fallen earth. This stick, which he had harvested from the surrounding burnt land, was a beacon of victory. The land itself could disappear, but the caboclo would remain. Beyond the convulsions of nature, beyond the frailty of the earth, was the soul of the native, in all its tranquility and resilience. So when the land itself sinks, only this soul floats, safe in the ark of his own chest, to which great hope always returns as soon as the cataclysm that drags the caboclo down comes to an end, sparing him.

After all, 'fallen land' could well be the very definition of the Amazon. Sometimes, in its alluvial soil, everything suddenly falters and sinks, but it then gradually reconstitutes itself. Here the land falls, there the

31. The money tree (*Pachira aquatica*).

land rises. The result is that, in this game of erosion and reclamation, man's effort is that of Atlas holding up the world, his struggle that of an inverted Sisyphus.

4. Hospitality

The stranger did not lodge in the street: but I opened my doors to the traveller.

Job 31:32

Reasoning inspired by fear went, as might have been expected, to the opposite extreme.
Alexandre Herculano, *History of the Inquisition in Portugal*

On August afternoons, a terral always blows, shaking the acuparana and inga trees of the floodplains, the purple-blossoming faveiras[1] and the whitish-blossoming jará palms of the igapós;[2] the fasciculated plumes of the urucuris[3] and caranás;[4] the serviceable laurels and abiuranas; and the uxis[5] and umaris[6] with their delicious fruits, lords of the dry land.

It is a useful wind. It spreads the undergrowth along the shore, and comes at the right time of year to relieve the oarsmen. Then the regatões[7]—who, in their igarités and galeotas,[8] go from port to port

---

1. A deciduous tree which grows well in inundated igapó and varzea forests. It has a strange green and red disc-shaped fruit and can be a source of wood (*Vatairea guianensis*).

2. Flooded forest, from Old Tupi for 'root forest'. Igapós are blackwater-flooded unlike the várzea, which are similar but whitewater-flooded.

3. A species of palm tree (*Attalea phalerata*).

4. A species of flowering plant in the family Arecaceae (*Mauritia carana*).

5. An evergreen tree with edible, nutritious fruit (*Endopleura uchi*).

6. A species of fruiting tree in the family Metteniusaceae (*Poraqueiba sericea*).

7. Either the owner of a travelling trade vessel or the vessel itself. These ships would travel around the Amazon selling a variety of products.

8. A ship which can either be rowed or use a sail, somewhere between the smaller montaria and the larger igarité.

speculating, leisurely and greedy, plying their trade—come up the river, their cloth swollen by the exceptional breeze. The sail on these vessels is like a cheek distended by an abscess; it does not have the graceful cut of marine sails, which are shaped into the elasticated wings of biguás,[9] and which, however they much puff out, remain smooth.

No matter: these little Noah's arks, even when stuffed to the brim with goods, glide along competing with the flight of the light black skimmer birds.

During this time the river is animated by new ornithological fauna. It is not only the placid herons or the screaming macaws that pass overhead; various montarias also parade by, spreading their adventitious wings to the north-easterly winds.

In the meantime, once the anemometric regime of the terral has passed, the wings are removed from the stump mast, and these, in turn, are detached from the carlings until the next monsoon. They will be raised again later, like the atavistic irruption of primordial organs that had lain dormant in the process of inheritance.

The caboclo perceives the slightest alteration in this animating breath with astonishing tact: he feels when it is about to cease, to increase in short or long bursts, or to sustain its gentle exhalation.

Having been assured by the pilot that I was certain to 'reach the top' of Varre-Vento before nightfall, I didn't pull over at Arauató. It would only be two hours: 'Just a bit longer, boss.' I acquiesced.

Then Manoel raised the sail, which, barely suspended, still gasped for breath, struggling against the whips of the fresh wind coming up from downriver. The cloth was fixed diagonally across the spar, waiting for the boom to be fastened. The rag seemed to have excited nerves; it pulsated in rapid waves resembling tetanus-induced spasms. Once the boom was fixed, the sail suddenly moulded itself into the shape of a cabocla dove's[10] chest; it became serene, full, and rigid. Soon water was lapping over the bow, and we were cruising along.

---

9. Indigenous name for the neotropic cormorant (*Nannopterum brasilianum*).

10. Regional name for a ruddy quail-dove (*Geotrygon montana*).

Toward the right bank were the islands of Benta, Trindade, Soriano and Cururú. The left bank had no such neighbours; it ran proudly, all high, in hardened marl with sections of alligator stone[11] in between, while on the opposite side, the Amazon, that eminent builder and demolisher, was filling the land downstream with cartloads of humus, sand, and clay it had dredged from further upstream. The islands could not really be made out from the firm shore; they looked like the same strip of land, an identical bar of muri grass, aningas,[12] and embaúba trees. Represented on maps, you can see all four; seen from the side they are indistinct from one another. They are like those sea walls through which the waters of the Mediterranean are constricted.

We had just passed Cainamã, a wide tract of land to the right, home to just one Black family. There were shacks disguised in the dense cocoa trees, at the foot of thin, quivering açaí trunks. Other signs of life included the cropfields, capoeira bush, igapós, and the small plots dotted with animals. Two metallic weathervanes, in prominent places, made pleasant sounds such as you might hear in more refined types of accommodation, with roof tiles and foie gras instead of shabby ubim palm leaves and dried fish.

This is how the ribbon of the coast was cut, and it continued through Amatari to Manaus. Amatari is a gully that is full of history, a palimpsest in clay and soil. A village populated by Mura people was once registered there, but was cleared to make room for the Mendes farm, and later it became a government agricultural colony. Between these two extremes—from maloca[13] to colonial hub, from the Indian

---

11. The popular name for a common type of rock in the Amazon. It has an irregular, greyish-black colour.

12. A climbing shrub with long, slender and strong roots that are used for making ropes, baskets and jamaxis (*Philodendron imbé*).

13. An ancestral long house used by indigenous peoples of the Amazon; also the settlement surrounding these—an indigenous village.

Manuel João[14] and Frei José das Chagas[15] to Colonel Bezerra—more than two and a half centuries passed. However, the curve of its development is capriciously undulating, bound by maximum and minimum lines which intertwine, making it irregular. At the current point on the curve, some fifty small houses, in the middle of an area of sparse tillage, define its state.

However, the succession of houses, farms, or smallholdings jutting out all along the shore, extreme points on a shared boundary, illustrate the rest of the country's ignorance, clouded as it is by the false vision of an uncultivated and uninhabitable Amazon. There are no rubber plantations in this area. So it is not just rubber that occupies, attracts, and retains capital and labour in Amazonas. Farming and cattle-raising, the 'two teats of the State', in the crude and magnificent phrase of that avaricious soldier and financier named Sully,[16] came to rest in the heart of these ravines.

The montaria, clinging to its sail, kept its prow on the desired course. A strange bird with invisible, strong wings, it turned responsively.

An hour of travelling.... The caboclo was locked in his usual silence, like a larva in a cocoon. In the evening the shadows grew funereally on the east side. To the west, the sun, upon its throne, wrapped itself in all the purples of Tyre and all the gold of the earth. As the montaria turned in this direction, one could have imagined that an Argonaut or a mad Englishman was carrying out legendary expeditions in the Amazon of today. The setting sun might be Colchis[17] for a moment,

---

14. An Indian of the Juma tribe who was captured at a young age in Maturá by the Mura tribe, who then raised him. As a result of his unusual intelligence and vivacity, he became the chief or *tuxaua* of his own tribe, founding a maloca. Later, in the middle of the last century, this became the Matari mission, a name taken from the nearby river.

15. A Carmelite missionary who helped create the village of São José de Matari. He spoke Old Tupi and used it to communicate with the indigenous population, after the fashion of José de Anchieta.

16. Maximilien de Béthune, Duke of Sully, Chief Minister of France from 1589–1611.

17. In Greek mythology, a wealthy, distant land which was the destination of the Argonauts.

or else the vanished Eldorado of Sir Walter Raleigh. In the prodigious light of the sunset, the landscape was fixed in the vivid lines of magnificent engraving.

With the threat of night, a gust of wind shifting the sail forced us into the channel of the Ilha Grande. As we entered the lee of Cururú the breeze dropped away, enchantingly unravelling the brown silk of the waters that it had rumpled. The ship's sail suddenly seemed seized with sleep or cold. It curled up. Lamentably, it fell into a coma, out of fear or shame at the effort it could no longer sustain.

The caboclo in the stern remained sceptical. He had been wrong! The Amazon is capable of anything: it deceives its own children. Thirty Augusts had scorched Manoel, and each time the same winds had exhaled their exasperated breath upon him. They were old hands at this, one at blowing, the other at being blown. So, inspired by consistency and sequence, the essential attributes of natural law, the caboclo thought that he had foreseen everything. And yet the sail fell, like a flag lowered in mourning of man's annihilated prescience.

Manoel gazed from north to east. The sail handle was completely loose and he held an oar in each hand. In the surveyed quadrant there were only glimpses of distant woods.... The caboclo took the bottomless bottle that was laid on the stern, and made a long, hoarse sound by blowing into it. He was honking to summon the wind. He blew harder on the raspy horn, but the ineffectual sounds did nothing to galvanise the doldrums of the afternoon. The wind had ceased, abruptly and apparently for good. Ducks flew in procession across the pearl tulle of the sky. The sun, abandoning its pompous solace like a cowardly king, showed only a segment of its red crown on the horizon. It was not long before it had completely immersed itself beneath the brown rim, above which the lights of the final scene of its magic show lingered, in celestial splendour. Finally it disappeared, while the genies of the night, garlanded with the gems of the stars, began to soak up the effluvia of the unfathomable darkness in the eternal and constellated round of the deserted heights.

Despite the fact that I was out in the open, by the river, a long way from Varre-Vento, I foolishly felt devastated, as though abandoned by a brother in the wilderness.

The caboclo remained silent, waiting for me to make a plan.

'Let's pull over to some shack on the Ilha Grande for the night', I mumbled under my breath in the wake of this setback.

The pilot, balancing on his hips, jumped into the forward cabin and, taking hold of the oar, began to scoop at the water with the rhythmic motion of a mechanical digger. The speed of the boat when rowed was markedly slower than the progress we had previously been making with the sail, unfurled and proud at the crisp kiss of the north-easterly wind. The montaria was like an ant that had leagues to travel. I leaned back in my seat.

The sail hung hopelessly from the mast. The brooch of the Pleiades pinned together the black silk of the evening. Other stellar families lit their fires on the banks of the Milky Way. The lanterns burning in the shacks in the distance also looked like stars rippling across the river.

The equatorial night eventually numbed us. Its feral glow had the narcotic effects of marijuana. My eyes began to close at the clopping of the oar and the gentle drifting of that cedar frame, which transported me with the gentle rocking of a cradle. And the surrounding vastness took on more limited dimensions, diminished, and finally ended altogether....

When the beating of the oar ceased, the rustling of the canaranas reeds on the montaria's hull, along with the barking of a dog, suddenly woke me up. The caboclo was adjusting the boat with a few oarstrokes. The memory of the meteorological disruption that had forced me to seek an unspecified and unforeseen shelter came back to me. The dog had stopped barking, magnetised by the sound of its name being called: 'Fox!... Fox!'

I jumped out and stood upon a slippery mound of tabatinga,[18] orienting myself with a view to climbing the slope. Steps had been

---

18. From the Tupi for 'white clay' or 'white soil', this refers specifically to the type of clay found at the bottom and on the borders of the rivers of the Amazon.

carved out of the crumbling slope of fallen earth. It was steep, with no handrail, and I climbed it panting with fatigue. I reached the top, between a thick clump of banana trees and a luxuriant calabash tree. Nearby, hidden in the middle of the bush, was the hut.

I stepped into the shadow of a man leaning against the calabash tree:

'Good evening! Who is it?'

A mellifluous voice answered me: 'Flor dos Santos.'

The nickname had the effect of a galvanic current in the network of my excited nerves. I already knew the name. It was that of a murderer, naturally feared by everyone. In the area around Itacoatiara and Autaz, this name was repeated in the squares and flour houses[19] with curiosity and dread. Two, three, or six deaths—that was the service record of this Troppmann[20] of the sertão. His unpunished crimes of uncertain number were seized on by popular belief and fear, leading people to come up with their own figures and stories. In the natural history of crime, Flor dos Santos stood out like a flower from the gardens of hell. That such a botanical delight and the title attributed to the greatest amongst men should be combined in the name of such a criminal![21]

I considered refusing his hospitality, but I felt it would have been foolish to go back. Besides, it was late.... The habit of travelling through the Amazonian Interior extinguishes fears, makes them seem vain, because one would not be able to take a single step there without overcoming them....

'This way,' the shadow told me, guiding me to the ranch's yard, adjacent to a lean-to.

---

19. These casas da farinha are where manioc flour is produced. They are vast sheds supported by columns of wood or masonry. In the centre of the house is a cassava tree, scraped by women sitting on the floor, usually armed with quicés (short knives).

20. Jean-Baptiste Troppmann: a famous French murderer born in Cernais (the Upper Rhine) in 1849 and executed in Paris on 19 January 1870.

21. A commentary making a great deal of the irony of the name Flor dos Santos (literally 'Flower of the Saints').

The villain went forth to fetch the lamp, pushing the japá[22] away from the doorframe. When he returned, the monster appeared to me in full detail. A tall, corpulent cabra[23] with a massive moustache on his broad face under thick hippopotamus-like nostrils. He really was a formidable creature; his physique was a match for his exploits. Just the right look for an *uomo delinquente*,[24] a constrictor like the green anaconda, poisonous like the timbó....[25]

While Manoel set up my hammock in the single room, I sat down in the yard on the trunk of an old palm tree. Flor dos Santos had come to the caboclo's aid. In the meantime, I gazed out at the night, attempting to make out particular colours in its vague, charcoal-sketch appearance.

The Amazonian night is always worthy of contemplation, whether or not there is moonlight. It is a voluptuous experience to be enveloped by it, to tear it apart with one's gaze and move into it wildly, straining through the shadows as if through an enchanted forest. Perhaps nowhere else provides these sensations, because no other country is so evocative, so full of contrast and novelty. Although taken as a whole, a dull melancholy, exuding from the bottom of a formidable igapó, hovers over it, in its details this gigantic swamp is astonishing. It surprises, alarms, and dazzles; it poisons and revivifies; it bewilders and soothes; it liberates and shackles. The Amazon...at once a virgin and a violated land, being suffocated and unveiled at the same time... capable both of arousing hatred and making you fall in love with it. It has made people abandon their families, relationships, and social

---

22. A sheet woven from palm leaves that serves as a door.

23. Literally 'goat', this term is slang for a daring or strong individual. The term also has racial associations and can mean 'mulatto'.

24. 'Criminal man', a categorical term of the Italian criminalist Cesare Lombroso for those with the proclivity to commit serious crimes, whose characteristics are supposedly inherited, the manifestation of kind of evolutionary throwback. Hence the zoological comparisons at play in the passage.

25. A rotenone-yielding plant that is very poisonous to fish. It is used for this purpose by the indigenous peoples of the Amazon. (*Lonchocarpus nicou*.)

standing, so that they can enjoy it in seclusion and solitude, even staying there as chieftains in remote indigenous villages.

'It's ready, boss', Manoel informed me.

Flor dos Santos and the caboclo oarsman were to take shelter under the gable roof. I went to bed. The andiroba oil lamp was lit and resting on a rough bench, next to the hammock.

Sleep did not arrive immediately: it simply could not. Myriad images swirled through my brain, in maddening rounds. I turned off the smoky lamp, which seemed to assist this dance of images with the mobility of its flame, not held in position by any kind of flue. Yet in the darkness, my brain seemed to light up. The images, though they were decreasing in number, became sharper. The murderer crowded out everything else.

Never in my life had I found myself in such a situation. My intrepidity—which the Amazonian interior makes commonplace, for it either eliminates the weak or, by strengthening them, instils in them a sense of self-worth which is only natural for self-preservation—faltered before this bizarre hospitality.

The fact is that I was at the mercy of Flor dos Santos. My sleep, under his roof, would be at his discretion; in his trap I would remain. Why had I not refused this lodging? Who had forced me into this state of fear? In an indescribable weakness of spirit, I came to throw foolish reproaches at myself: 'I should go back! I should go back! What for? What an unpleasant situation...I chose to do it...It didn't have to be like this....' It felt as if I was speaking aloud words which were only imprinted in the negative of my brain.

Finally, I felt my eyelids, which had been repelling each other, begin to pull together. Sleep was about to conquer all, defeating any surviving resistance in a final assault, when a sound in the doorway roused me completely. I could distinguish it in the dim light of the starry night. It was a man coming in...it was Flor dos Santos! I could see him cautiously twisting his body to ease himself through the doorway, which had only been half open.

I did not move, but my impression was that I had made a start. As one of our internal vital functions, the circulation of the blood is a fact of life, but it was only at that moment that I perceived it, because the flow had stopped, frozen. Terrified, I wanted to scream. Should I re-... react? I remained paralysed. Flor dos Santos was taking increasing caution, advancing towards me. Evidently, he thought I was asleep. My eyes must have been hideous, popping out of their sockets because I was looking so intently. My constricted throat would not even let out a whimper. Everything in me was keenly intent upon the strange visitor. I can't say that I was thinking, because the thoughts never fully formed, trying to shuffle along like terrified spectators pressing towards the exit of a theatre on fire.

The bandit approached ever more cautiously. In one hand he held a pointed knife which flashed at me as if it had already been swiftly wedged up to the handle into my dying chest. The familiar steel caused my muscles to feel the chill of death. Then the complete breakdown of my personality took place. Frozen still, I felt as if I were falling through an ice-cold vacuum. The terror, the stupid cowardice had reached the highest note in its indecipherable scale.

Flor stopped by the bench. I saw that he had put down his knife there. In a flash I checked once again that he had abandoned the blade and was returning to the door. In a second flash I understood everything.

With my miserably frayed nerves and the unbearable muscular tension of my entire being, which if it had obeyed the soul would have been reduced to a speck of dust, I arrived at a simple explanation for this scene, one that was like something out of Edgar Allan Poe.

I ran my hand across the seat to reassure myself. Calmness flooded my poor mind, shipwrecked by this one single fact: a murderer, armed, coming into the room of a man lying asleep at night.

My heart's hasty palpitations grew still. Flor dos Santos was already on his way out and I had just spotted the roll of tobacco and the knife with which to cut it on the bench. He had brought it in for me, in fatherly and affectionate care for the one he was providing shelter to.

I ran my hand across my forehead, dewy as if I had been out in the open all night.

In the morning Flor dos Santos offered me coffee. He apologised for the inferior quality of the sugar, which was brown; and, he asked, indicating the bundle on the bench, 'Did you enjoy the tobacco?'

'Oh! very much', I replied.

I asked him if he had planted it himself.

'It's this one here.' And, showing me a row of dried leaves stuck in the thatch of the ranch's deck, the grinning killer said: 'I grew it all right. Who else could it have been?'

This tiger's hospitality was positively Middle Eastern. The dog from the night before, placid and mangy, was brushing against my legs.

'Get out, Fox! Get out!' Then this Arab of the sertão led his Molossian guard dog away, so that his guest would not be bothered even by the gentleness of this animal.

This wrongdoer, a refugee from human law, exercised a divine law in his own abode. Here, the reprobate was a patriarch....

5. The Eldest of the Mura

To scorched feet they cling,
countless generations lying in ashes and worms.

Almeida Garrett, 'A morte'

To look at the physical map of the Amazon is to see the continuous vascular network in the epidermis of the lamina of an inequilateral leaf. This image, in all its striking generality, is quite faithful in its details. The Amazon, the river, is like the woody beam of the main vein, and the tributaries are the secondary veins, curving outwards. These branch out prodigiously into the exceptional and unique hydrographic network that knits together the parenchyma of the regions of the forest. The secondary vein of the Urubu does not issue directly from the Amazon, but lies between the leaves of the Saracá lake, at the foot of Silves, where Inglês de Souza rebelliously donned the mantle of an unsettled missionary whose sinful embrace with a woman culminated in the 'confirmation' of Man.[1]

Struggling to descend the last steps of an immense staircase, when the course settles down and spreads out into the valley, the Urubu immediately tries to find the final channel for which it is destined.

---

1. A reference to 'O missionário', a story by Inglês de Souza, a pioneer of Brazilian naturalist fiction. The work originated from a short story called 'O Sofisma do Vigário [The Vicar's Sophistry]', and explores the complex relationship between the titular young priest, Antônio de Morais, who arrives in Silves, and Clarinha, a mameluca from the impoverished region where he is assigned to carry out his missionary work.

Then, after leaping over the last escarpments of the Guiana Shield, it emits the strands of the furos.

This river of murky brown waters, trapped between steep cliffs, which engineers—in industrial fantasies, which may well come true—plan to divert into a dam, flows through history with blood-reddened waters, between outbursts of fire. It is as though the lines from 'Childe Harold's Pilgrimage'[2] were written especially for it: 'Thy tide wash'd down the blood of yesterday.' Two and a half centuries ago, when its name first became known, it was as the scene of carnage. They corrupted the original name, which was onomatopoeia for its rumbling waterfalls: Bururú. They killed its riverside populations, in a horrific revenge-driven raid ordered by a certain Governor Ruy Vaz de Siqueira....

At times, igarité canoes have chased escaped Blacks, cabanos,[3] or Urubuguayans[4] in its sepulchral waters. In its mysterious seclusion, it has always attracted scorpions and frail reptiles like a dark cave. This sepulchral, remote, abandoned place served as a nucleus for Indian races, harboured political insurgents, and became a safe haven for slaves escaping from their irons and from the lash of the 'bacalhau'.[5]

Indigenous maloca villages, parishes, and mocambos:[6] everything has disappeared into the Urubú of today, which, like a mysterious and tragic river of legend, flows on in a country of ruins and silence. That is why, mindful of the terrifying memory of martyrdoms recalled in dark and chaotic tales of persecutions and killings, perhaps it is more

---

2. A narrative poem by Lord Byron published between 1812 and 1818.

3. Bands of rebels, notable for taking part in the Cabanagem revolt. The name comes from the cabana huts they would live in.

4. Namely inhabitants of the banks of the river Urubu; a similar formulation to Paraguay and Uruguay (both from the Guaraní).

5. A type of whip used by slavemasters.

6. Also called a quilombo (mocambos are generally smaller, and quilombos can contain mocambos), these were communities formed by escaped slaves in the forest. See R. Price, *Maroon Societies: Slave and Rebel Communities in the Americas* (Baltimore, MD: Johns Hopkins University Press, 1981) for a lengthy study on the subject.

prudent to advance toward the civilisation of the Amazon with the cautious disposition of the antennae that form the furos.

It was because of one of these furos, the Cainamansinho, that curiosity had gotten the better of me and I decided to visit this dark river of dismal repute.

It was April, and the route must have been rough, as it so often was, swamped by the flood which had already submerged the flood-plains and the lowlands.

In the dry season the furo is a parched channel, but in the flood it is like a swollen vein. When in the latter state, the canoe shoots through it like an arrow through the forest, caught up in the frenzied passage of a river from source to mouth. The only things to be avoided are the branches and vines that scrape the seat of the montaria. The liana vines are terrible. They seem to be specifically made to punish imprudent passers-by. With this in mind the 'chameleon' vine sharpens its teeth; the 'wait first', the tiririca and the cat's claw creepers[7] sharpen their thousands of spikes and tines.

But the journey was beautiful. In the complete shade of the enclosed forest, the furo crept along in a soft murmur. At one moment it suddenly bumped into a tree trunk, foamed up, and then continued on, spilling out later into the marsh. This soaked up the coarse, tangled hair of branches suspended above it. These branches of cacao trees, socorós[8] and oruás leaned over the water, meaning that an awning stretched across the furo, turning it into a delightfully green route, with uninterrupted shade.

In the furo we were surprised by the intimacy of the forest, for, knowing itself to be impenetrable by land, it did not care, nor did it even perceive, that the strong current was seeping through its entrails, devouring it from within its hidden and leafy interior. The birds that

---

7. A rapidly growing climbing vine with yellow flowers (*Dolichandra unguis-cati*).

8. An evergreen shrub or tree with an orange-red globose fruit (*Mouriri guianensis*).

populated it did not care either. The japiins[9] and japós[10] twittered on the high branches of some enormous kapok tree,[11] woodpeckers hammered on the trunks, sururinas[12] and macucauas[13] hooted, a drowsy tamburú-pará[14] fell asleep....

Half an hour later, the furo shot into a small lake, round and burnished like a glazed faience ware dish. And what is more, near where a Victoria waterlily opened its huge circular leaves, some Japanese artist had painted monstrous nymphs on the faience.... The lake was completely full of uaupés,[15] mururés,[16] sapê-mirins[17] and canaranas, well suited to the palates of manatees. Almost its entire surface was covered with marvellous plants, across which light-footed jacanas[18] strolled.

The metallic cries of horned screamers[19] sounded out.... The canoe's bowman had called the huge floating lily by the vulgar appellation 'alligator's oven'.[20] Indifferent to its beauty, he plunged the paddle of the oar into the soft leathery leaves of the lily. It had been floating alone, basking in the glory of being the queen of a vast

---

9. The yellow-rumped cacique (*Cacicus cela*).

10. The Amazonian Oropendola (*Psarocolius yuracares*).

11. A tropical tree of the order *Malvales* and the family *Malvaceae*. The tree is cultivated for its cottonlike seed fibre, known simply as kapok (*Ceiba pentandra*).

12. The little tinamous (*Crypturellus soui*).

13. The undulated tinamous (*Crypturellus undulatus*).

14. A nunbird, one of the *Monasa* genus of puffbird.

15. A gigantic water lily (*Victoria amazonica*).

16. A water lily with a white flower (*Nymphaea amazonum*).

17. A type of grass also known as West Indian foxtail (*Andropogon bicornis*).

18. Jesus birds or lily trotters (*Jacanidae*). Rangel also mentions 'piaçocas' here, but this appears to refer to the same family of birds, so we must imagine a variety of jacanas.

19. (*Anihima cornuta*).

20. A vernacular name for the *Victoria amazonica* mentioned above.

plant species, and had now been decapitated by an executioner. It remained afloat, even though torn apart, when, pulling away from the sapé-mirins and canaranas on the banks, we entered the forest again. The water rippled, disturbed by the oarstrokes. Dragonflies scribbled passageways through the air, gleaming.

It was no longer a well-defined river channel. The water invaded the undergrowth at will, in a sprawling, deep flood. As far as the eye could see, through the canopies and between the trees, it was an ocean, but one without ripples, waves, or foam, with the cold glow of black agate. In the flood, which penetrated everything, only the most astute would have been able to keep track of where they were heading.

Inundated by the water, the forest was as though cloaked in mourning, wrapped up in the pain of a bereavement, embraced by a spectre.... Not even the briefest chirp of a pipira[21] could lend any cheer to those dark and fierce surroundings. A rare splash of otters diving, the occasional tumble of a piece of fruit.... This watery solitude was quite disheartening. As soon as you entered it, you were struck by the impression of already being hopelessly lost in a labyrinth. The pounding of the oars in the water resounded cavernously, as if it were at the bottom of a deep grotto, one that was freezing, damp, and filled with bats. That sea, that vast expanse of water, conjured up nightmarish fears: anacondas tangled in submerged trunks, ready to enwrap their prey in an iron grip.

Suddenly, as it passed by an impressive muiratinga tree,[22] the furo became clearly defined again, like a fistula boring from the abscess of the lake into the forest, obscured, creeping lazily, chasing stingrays and electric eels, under the dome of branches and through this nave of a temple whose patron saint was Our Lady of Solitude.

The channel now flowed more freely, in a capricious tear. Because fewer branches and vines hindered it, the furo finally gained more freedom. It began to revel, enjoying itself, setting aside any bad luck

---

21. A bird in the genus *thraupis*.

22. A large deciduous tree, which can grow up to 40m tall (*Maquira coriacea*).

or doubts, sliding through the groove in the curved, sinusoidal, slippery embankment.

Tired of resisting, the forest left the field free for the indiscreet intruder. I was thus riding through a maze toward the gloomy river on my montaria, when, disguised behind the inga trees, I unexpectedly came across a farm besieged by capoeira.

Since it made sense to stop in order to obtain information from the resident about the state of the route and whether the Urubu was still far away, I disembarked. Some dogs, which had rushed over barking, were quieted down by someone I could not see. A jacuaru lizard deftly fled through some dry leaves upon hearing my steps.

I followed the path lined with sprawling pega-pinto.[23] A small and battered field of joão-gome[24] and caruru[25] surrounded a simple canopy without any walls. At an angle to the ranch was a crumbling clay oven. A lacerated tipiti[26] hung from a stake and there were some cold ashes in the moquém grill. Around the yard there were ipadu trees,[27] some mastruço[28] and papaya trees and clumps of 'capim santo'....[29] A cotton bush spread out its snowy hoods to the sun. Some distance away, a superb guajará[30] imperiously raised its fringed fronds, bathed in bright light.

---

23. Punarnava or spreading hogweed, a species of plant in the 'four o'clock' family, popular in various herbal medicine traditions (*Boerhavia diffusa*).

24. Fameflower, an evergreen subshrub with small flowers (*Talinum paniculatum*).

25. (*Amaranthus blitum* subsp. *oleracea*).

26. A cylindrical straw-woven container in which manioc is squeezed before being baked.

27. One of the four cultivated plants in the family Erythroxylaceae, famous for its psychoactive alkaloid: cocaine (*Erythroxylum coca*).

28. Jesuit's tea or Mexican tea, an annual or short-lived perennial herb (*Dysphania ambrosioides*).

29. A tree with edible fruit in the family Sapotaceae (*Dysphania ambrosioides*).

30. (*Chrysophyllum venezuelanense*).

What sort of creature lived in this pitiful den, at this mid-station? What type of Cearense would be willing to take refuge in this place, almost entirely forgotten, this nemoral recess of helplessness and misery? Only some deserter or Indian, I thought; no sooner had I thought this than a hideous shape stirred in a corner, rising up.

I began to examine it, stunned. She was a woman, the colour of raw clay, enormous and adipose. Her undignified nudity, which was repulsively in evidence, was wrapped in a short rag. This hung on her monstrous belly like a skirt, from her hips down to her knees. Her dull eyes were barely visible in her earthy face. Her mouth was withered and without lips. Her hair was piled, very thin, on her receding forehead. On her face, which was cruelly flat, the skin was all wrinkled, like the epicarp of a ripe genipa fruit. Her neck was covered with disgusting hides, over which hung a white muiraquitã[31] pendant on a tucum thread. Her bowed legs could hardly support the heap of sagging, scabby lard. They were deformed and twisted like two envireira tree trunks.[32]

'*Reiké rewapika*',[33] said the abominable creature, indifferent to the cloud of mosquitos that covered her. And, In a strange nasal murmur, she added: '*Maáta remunhã reikú?*'[34]

I did not understand, nor did I know how to answer this apparition. Soon I was just about able to understand that the ranch's inhabitant was a Mura Indian. She was so old that she must have been the eldest survivor of this diminished race.

In remote times, her people had spread from the tops of the Parintins Mountains to the mouth of the Jutaí River. But the lies and violence of the deceitful and wicked caríua[35] had exterminated their ancestors. Today, in Pantaleão and other parts of Autaz, there are still a few scant denizens of the tribe—miserable riffraff riddled with

---

31. An amulet carved from stone, often in the shape or a frog or a bird.

32. A type of tree in the family Malvaceae (*Luehea ochrophylla*).

33. Nheengatu or Modern Tupi for 'Come in and take a seat'. Transliteration updated from the original, with thanks to Eduardo de Almeida Navarro.

34. 'What are you doing?'

35. White man; Christian.

alcohol, thieves and vagrants, under the harmless supervision of Colonel Barroncas. Yet they were once a strong and warlike people. Their submission to the 'white man' dates back just over a century. Since then, this enslaved race has withered and almost died out. What was not transfused, absorbed by the 'white man', was worn down in ravine villages under the despotism of the Directors, the deceit and the fervid fanaticism of the missionaries, and the weakened internal government of the impotent tuxauas.[36] Of this humble remnant, this hag who looked at me was the oldest and most hideous example.

In this secluded spot which she had chosen by instinct, there was no way that Death, diligently harvesting the world, would have time to come and collect her from her secret shelter. The Indian woman had, of course, been forgotten at the edge of this furo which had burrowed and tangled its way into the forest. A solitary soul, so far away! And the convoluted skein of watery threads one must follow in order reach this monster is beyond all comprehension!

The old woman was not able to relax and enjoy what little life was left to her. Her gnarled fingers dug the pits for the manioc; they filled these up from the pot; they pruned the shoots of the meagre tobacco plant at her feet; they pulled up the manioc roots, put them in water to stew, grated them, dried out the dough, and put it in the oven to bake. In her old age, life was still a struggle to be endured and overcome.

The only survivor of the extinct malocas, she had been witness to the misfortunes of so many of her brethren. How many times, just how many, had the moon—the maternal Jaci[37]—aroused her adoration, at the arrival or departure of the night, kissing the tufts of the branches with her white lip? Those she had nurtured as children, those she had watched die in the wars, those who had exhaled whimpers, moans, and confessions, in ecstasy, in her warm bosom, no longer had a place in the confines of her memory. This ancient, shapeless creature probably had neither memories nor nostalgia. Her brain had been filled

---

36. A type of tribal chief.

37. An indigenous moon goddess.

to the brim with such a surfeit of past that it was now an oppressed mass in which no imaginative spark had occurred for a long time.

The woman was a vegetable. She just lived on—stupid, heavy, and inert. She took care of herself like a plant obeying its geotropism, its roots and rootlets seeking nitrogen and moisture, its leaves exposed to the air for chlorophyll exchange. With the base determinism of the lower lifeforms, the banal yet powerful instinct of self-preservation!

But this grubby hydropic harpy must at one point have cut a graceful figure, as supple as the mauritia palms, her hair the black and lustrous colour of the ani cuckoo. Her eyes two night-time lagoons containing Iaras.... Her voice would have imitated the song of the bewitched uirapuru.[38] She would have loved, she would have an anxious heart, she would have dreamed.... Now, as the abject detritus of a degraded race, her life was simpler. There were no sentimental complications, no vertiginous thoughts. In this obese and hideous body, her heart was nothing but a box of broken valves, her brain just the indispensable housing of an increasingly dull consciousness.

What more could be required of this sacred remnant, stubbornly continuing to represent a great people, long buried in the igapós of a vast region? Discarded in her hovel, this Indian Medusa was a venerable relic. She was protected in the reliquary of her tutelary forest, which preserved her in an illusory state of immortality. We usually attribute the prize of such immortality to those of refined subjectivity, but nature, doing its best to grant it objectively, had handed the laurels to this old Indian woman lost on the edge of the furo, naked and fat, stupid and torpid, like a croaking frog on the edge of the marsh.

Hanging from the eaves of the ranch, a hive of jatis worked feverishly, buzzing industriously. A dog, almost skeletal in form, tenderly licked the leprous, unsteady legs of this stupefied monarch, who sat

---

38. A name derived from Tupi applied to various members of the Pipiridae family. In this case it applies to the musician wren or organ wren (*Cyphorhinus arada*). These are well-known for having an extraordinary variety of song patterns and are the subject of numerous legends and fables revolving around their musical prowess. Notably, the Brazilian composer Heito Villa-Lobos wrote a symphonic poem called *Uirapuru: O passarinho encantado* (*The Enchanted Little Bird*).

down on the ground like an imbecile; another guard dog stood utterly fixated on a dung heap....

Leaving the rest of my lunch to this everlasting carcass, the leftovers of her nation, I got back into the canoe. I was fascinated by my newfound reluctance to reach the river, which had been gloomy and sullen ever since the Portuguese Capitan Favella[39] had terrorised it with slaughter. That river had mirrored the flames of three hundred burned malocas and—the drain of a historic abattoir—carried away the blood from the chests and flanks of seven hundred pure-blooded Brazilians.

---

39. Pedro da Costa Favella. A military captain involved in an episode where the Tupinambás accepted the help of the Portuguese to repel the assaults of their enemies, the Caboquenas and Guadavenas. The resulting expedition led by Favella consisted of 34 canoes with 300 Tupinambás and 4 companies of Portuguese troops, under the command of 4 infantry captains and other non-commissioned officers. After having fought the battle and defeated these their enemies, it transpired that 700 Indians had died, 400 had been taken prisoner, and over 300 villages had been set alight.

6. A Good Man

If they are without understanding,
they cannot be considered malicious....

Desiderius Erasmus, *In Praise of Folly*

Having crossed the Santo Antonio Lake in one leap at the short triangular section, the trek continued on through a vast tract of land, which had to be crossed on the same bearing.

During the night, heavy rain and thunder had flooded the group's tapiri cabins, washing them away. The storm had descended, accompanied by the bizarre sound made by branches being shaken and splintered by violent gusts. Thuds, shrieks, squawks, bangs, chirping—all these familiar nocturnal noises were replaced by one single roar. The whole forest had exploded into it, its intricate and unstable edifice shaken. The Amazon rainforest is so unique! Even though it is so tall and dense, it does not have the strength to stand upright on its own, and is as brittle as glass. When one of its trees falls, it drags its companions down with it. A gust of wind can blow it to pieces. As it staggers, betraying its frailty, adventitious roots, lianas, and sapomemas support it unsteadily....

With the light of dawn, however, it all came to an end. Now all that was left were the coarse droplets falling from glistening leaves, weeping away the water that had drenched them. The twitterings, trillings and pipings of invisible birds greeted the fresh dawn.

The dewy forest, which had trembled in terror, grew quiet, drying up and laughing at the light that smiled upon it. Like one who had been possessed, plagued by demons, only to feel blessed at the exorcism of the dawn.

Once the light was bright enough to break through the palisades of the wood, after having been served a bowl of broth into which two pieces of peccary had been stuffed, we left the rough settlement. We went on to resume the work we had left the day before at Stake 515.

Taking advantage of the opening that had already been made in the trail, a man had left a trap there. We found the discharged rifle among the ferns and quiobas.[1] In a frenzy of joy, we all surrounded the magnificent tapir that the weapon had killed. The tapir was a little way ahead and just off the trail, having made a short and futile attempt at escape. He was reclining, as if asleep, his belly hanging open, on a sumptuous bed pompously appointed with delicate mosses and white grubs. No Queen's corpse had ever rested on such a pampered carpet. The animal had been brought down simply by running into a thin string. A fearsome steeple-chase runner—who normally never stumbled, navigating effortlessly between trees—had been knocked down by something so small. The lightest of touches on the string had set off the gunshot, according to the diabolical design of the contraption. The man who was carrying the reference beacons stayed behind to strip the beast of its hide and then quarter it while we continued on to that last numbered stake.

From that point onward, the forest grew denser. It was no longer a flimsy thicket, but a tight weave which the machetes and scythes would have a hard time breaking through.

In this area, a human track could only be found when walking along trails to some remote reservoir, lake, or igarapé. All that stood out were the tracks of jaguars, pacas, and wily, scurrying deer.

From time to time, Brazil nut trees, the castanheira excelsa,[2] majestic in name and appearance, came to dominate the fabric of the forest. Around them there remained scattered husks, broken in the last harvest. The heaps of shells were a testament to the extractive

---

1. A shrub, originally native to Africa.

2. *Bertholletia excelsa*—castanheira (or castanheira-do-Brasil) is the trade name; migrant workers who gathered the nuts were known as castanheiros.

exploitation that had animated the sertão, set in motion by some dry linear and angular data on an official plan.

Once the fruits had fallen from those monumental fronds, the work was over. The forest was temporarily abandoned as unproductive. Man would return once the produce ripened on the trees once again. Then, neither malaria, nor the risk of being knocked in the head by a nutshell[3] falling suddenly, could keep the caboclo from harvesting these nuts. Their boss, in some lake or nearby igarapé, would keep watch, waiting with leonine determination for the valuable product to arrive. A barrel of Brazil nuts would be worth a litre of brandy. By poisoning the Mura, the Cearense increased their profits. But they were exploited in turn, making rich men of the Portuguese or Jews who had hired them in the city.

The transit[4] had been centred on the stake, next to a delirious whirlwind of cypress branches and twigs. A kapok tree rose beyond the greenish canopies of the other trees, which were tall but dwarfed next to that monster which had buttress roots for shoes. With the collimination line at the base of the survey marker carefully aligned on the previous stake using the locking screw and the fine adjustment screw, the measuring operation continued. The lens that had been previously pointed backwards was now facing forwards to the next stake.

The dry leaves made the floor into a thick and wide doormat that tore and fell to tatters at the footsteps of the busy men of the group.

As it went on, the trail took a straight but lengthy route. One would imagine that the fabled Cobra Grande had set off in this direction, suspiciously attempting to cover its scent, crawling over thick trunks and thin branches, proceeding onwards indifferently, with its leaden scales, its thick coils unfolding on the soft soil of the lowlands, the mud of the igapós, the current of the igarapés and the elevated terra firma.

---

3. Not such a comical proposition—the outer shells, each containing between twelve and twenty Brazil nuts, can be up to 2kg in weight.

4. An American type of theodolite popular in Amazonian expeditions during the period.

The sun was shining through the canopy of branches. It was like a light playing on the carvings and reliefs of the ancient, damp arches of the cloister of a ruined Gothic abbey. The surveying operation we were engaged in progressed slowly. All that could be heard was the beating of irons striking the branches, stems, and leaves.

Suddenly, as the scythes and hatchets cut through the thick sheets of taquaris and tiriricas to either side of the narrow path, the trail came up against the thick trunk of a murumuru tree, whose opulent crown of palms bowed toward the ground. The axeman quickly began to attack it. Knowing the fibre of the astrocaria to be as steely as the axe itself, I lit my cigarette and waited for the stiff palm tree to fall.

Near me stood the man whose job it was to carry the instrument. He had a scraggly beard on his thin chin, a face with prominent cheekbones, a dull lymphatic complexion and, among his sickly features, the bulbous, expressionless eyes of a dead fish.

As a beam of light streamed through the theodolite, he opened the sunshade to protect himself. At this movement, the man's small cotton shirt opened up, baring his bald and dark chest. Right next to his heart I could make out an enormous scar. Unable to contain myself, I asked him what could possibly have caused such a wound.

'In happened back in Ceará, sir', he replied.

'But how?' I inquired, overwhelmed by a compulsion to communicate, as the edge of the axe struck at and gouged into the ancient murumuru.

'I can't even begin to tell you, doctor.'[5] He then continued in a solemn outburst, delivered in a type of prosody peculiar to the speech patterns of an old sertanejo. 'This happened in the year of three eights.[6] I lived in Granguê and made my livelihood from planting cotton, as well as farming. Once in a while, I went to Aracati or União to sell tobacco and leather. Colonel Távora, my boss, was very fond of me. When he

---

5. The man refers to the narrator as a doctor because of the engineering degree required for this type of surveying. Elsewhere in the story he does the same for other professional qualifications.

6. Presumably a colloquial expression for the year 1888.

needed a man, he sent for me straight away and handed me a small carbine, a weapon we used to call a bug gun! One time he told me to get rid of a guy who had gone round the bend, right next to the carnauba tree on the way back from the road with the mandacarus.[7] It only took one shot!'

'And it was never reported to the police?'

'Who would dare, doctor?' quipped the young man.

Alligators bellowed in the distance, filling the woods with a thunderous sound.

'He was a good man, Colonel Távora, and an important man. He was talked about in those parts like no other! He was very old. By the time of the drought of seventy-seven[8] he already had male children. Despite this, he had just married a robust young girl, Dona Maroca do Crato, daughter of Major Fulgêncio Cabeça de Sola. She was so pretty! Her face was as white as cotton, and her teeth were like two rows of little pearls. This fellow I'd picked off in the carnauba palm grove, had come from the capital to be a public prosecutor. He was a good-looking lad and knew how to sing some great songs. Any night when there was a party at the farm, the little doctor was always there. Apparently, he was trying to lead Dona Maroca astray, and that's why the Colonel decided to flip this bug on his back.'

'Was this the only man the Colonel ordered you to kill?'

The tabaréu, the 'porter of the scope'[9] as he used to call himself, drew a meaningful smile on his bloodless face.

'Well, continue the story,' I said, somewhere between interested and distracted.

---

7. A cactus native to Brazil. It has wide flowers and a deep red fruit that is considered extremely tasty. (*Cereus jamacaru*.)

8. This is a reference to the Grande Seca of 1877–1878, which, along with other similar events, was ultimately the cause of much of the internal migration from Ceará into Amazonas. It was the largest drought in Brazilian history and led to the deaths of around 500,000 people.

9. I.e. the person charged with carrying the transit theodolite.

The axe continued to strike the palm tree with repeated but halting blows. The shrieks of macaws reached us from the heights.

Straightening the brim of his miriti palm hat, the man resumed the narrative with naive sincerity and even a hint of pride at remembering, in his cruel exile in Amazonas, these events from his beloved Ceará which interested the 'white man' so much.

'The thing is...Dona Maroca, the Colonel's wife, was "positive" she knew what had happened and that it was I who had taken out the Public Prosecutor. One day, because of the need to prepare for elections in the town, the government sent for the Colonel. When he sent his footman to saddle up the quartau,[10] a famous quartau with a honey-coloured roan coat, he handed me the carbine as collateral and recommended that every night I go and watch the casa grande and sleep in the flour store, which was empty. So that's what I did. Early in the morning I left the granary and went to look after my vegetables. On the third night the Colonel was away, I headed straight to the barn, but I was feeling scared and started to get quite flustered. I felt a spectre creep across my back. I kissed my scapular three times. All the same, I had promised the Colonel, I was still going to go. It was an ugly night. The wind, which would suddenly come to a stop, rattled the branches of the angicos[11] and joazeiros[12] in the caatinga[13] that I had to cross. It took a lot of effort to get through it. I could see the barn and, like a mocó[14] hiding between rocks, I scurried inside. I was very upset. My teeth were chattering. I don't think the cold was coming from the outside, it was inside me. Ah, doctor! I remember it well.

---

10. A small yet robust horse.

11. A perennial shrub or tree (*Parapiptadenia rigida*).

12. A fruiting tree in the buckthorn family found in the caatinga shrubland of the sertão (*Ziziphus joazeiro*).

13. Rough and scraggly shrubland in the sertão.

14. A rock cavy, a large rodent found in dry rocky areas (such as the sertão). Since they like to reside in stony mountainsides and hills, presumably the sight of one taking shelter in a crevice would be quite familiar to a sertanejo.

The moon was round like a beiju[15] and the evening star must have been fading away. All of a sudden I found myself grabbed by two cabras, who tied me up and dragged me into the yard, right under an oiticica tree at the foot of the waterhole. And who should be there watching, doctor? Dona Maroca, who, seeing me, called out the name of the Public Prosecutor and ordered: "I want to see this evil cabra's heart. Tear it out right now...." Ah! Doctor, I collapsed. I was done for. All I could do was to pray to São Bomfim do Icó; I felt a parnaíba machete ploughing through my chest. But they didn't get to finish the job, doctor. Just then, the old man, the Colonel, with his chiquerador whip in his hand, jumped up close to me, like a jaguar. The cabras fled; Dona Maroca went pale and limp, as though she had seen a ghost, while he untied the knots that were holding me down. He had appeared so suddenly. A man as distrustful as a demon, wanting to be "positive" himself, he had been spying on everything from behind the mofumbo bushes. He had immediately realised that Dona Maroca was taking revenge on me for the death of the Public Prosecutor. Advancing towards his wife, quick as a preá,[16] the Colonel subdued her and then ordered me from behind her back, "positive", to rip her heart out...'

The porter of the scope paused for a moment, which distressed me. A strange spark brought life to his dull eyes. Then he added, 'I did it, doctor...the Colonel was my boss...the little woman squealed like a stuck pig. Her heart was so warm in my hands...it was like seeing a goat's innards. The Colonel, giving the order to bury everything, left the yard with such sobs that you would have thought the world had ended....'

And then the narrator, instinctively trying to close his shirt where I had seen the scar caused by the terrible butchery, reflected, 'Never mind! He was a good man, the Colonel; he always helped me when I got into fights and with all the troubles I had in my life.' And he confirmed, in conclusion: 'a man known as the Colonel, and a damned clever one, he could write even when he was lying down!'

---

15. A crêpe made from tapioca.

16. The Brazilian guinea pig (*Cavia avereá*).

The axes ceased; the murumuru thudded to the ground on the trail, like a dead body laid out by a single sharp blow to the back of the head.

7. Obstinacy

I've seen them among us, in our homeland,
Dying of homesickness.

Tristan Corbière, *Les Amours Jaunes*

At the end of June, the Amazon River shows the first unmistakable signs of a reduction in its flow. It begins to dwindle subtly. Sometimes it lingers on, still at full capacity, repentant, its strength replenished. And then the poor, depleted river starts to lay bare the streams and rocks of the rapids. It threatens to dry up. Huge stretches of beach emerge around the islands or along the higher banks of the river, where turtles nest and can be flipped.[1] Everything the water had recently flooded now takes on the appearance of a barrier inaccessible to the attacks of the flood to come. Thus fortified, it hunkers down, stretching out in lines of barbicans along the immense, besieged ramparts of the endless citadel. Muri grass covers the slopes revealed by the ebbing of the water. Cautious steamers travel further upriver, avoiding the shores, now full of new hazards....

The short summer scorches the crops. In one month of sunshine everything is desiccated, as if licked by a vast flame. There is plenty of water left for the large ocean liners, but there is no way of using it for irrigation, which would save the crops. The difference in level between the maximum ebb and the flood brings the water to a height beyond

---

1. Viração—a term for the capture of turtles by turning them on their backs and tying up their legs. The word is also used to designate the spots on the riverside where this would occur.

that established by the pneumatic principle that governs the pumps. This impedes any easy use of the water that flows, muddy and useless, alongside the parched floodlands and plains. The earth is tortured like Tantalus.[2] At the lower edge of the slopes, it can drink from the river, still wide, flowing and deep, but at the top of them everything is dried up, agonising with thirst. The colonia, pampuã,[3] and mium grasses of the fields, turning yellow, tend to die. The fruit trees become infirm and wither, and the fields dry up discouragingly. When the rains come, they provide some dampness, postponing the danger with which the drought had threatened everything.

When the time is right, the return of the flood is announced without any drama or any sudden rush of lapping water, although it will later climb the banks, drown all the floodplains, and cover the rocky outcrops with its surging currents. On the sandy beaches, the river also marks its upward movement imperceptibly, each day gaining an inch on the previous day's level. It goes on like this, from moment to moment; the invisible growth of a living organism. At times it will have to stop in its tracks, momentarily running out of steam or gathering its forces in preparation for the monstrous expansion of the flood.

It is then that the great timbers set off down the river, lazy and slow, bumping along, rattling their way blindly and carelessly, jostled by whirlpools, trapped at the edges of backwaters....

These logs will eventually be split into doorframes, slats, planks, and stilt-legs. Some of the giant pieces of wood which make their sluggish way downriver are almost completely submerged. Only the branches or the roots unravel, like claws, through the brocade of the waters within which these proud and majestic giants are entwined.

And then the 'cedar fishing' season begins. These wandering trees, which fall from rafts on the Solimões, are snatched up by riverside

2. The mythological figure Tantalus was famously made to stand in a pool of water which would immediately recede whenever he tried to take a drink to quench his thirst. This is the source of the verb 'to tantalise'.

3. A weed belonging to the grass family. Frequently used as animal feed. (*Panicum plataginum* or *Urochloa plantaginea*.)

inhabitants. As word spreads about the valuable floating fragments from afar, they set out to catch these fugitives. Reaching one, they tie a tow rope to it and pull it over the edge of a nearby bank.

Along with the trunks come floating green islands of canaranas and aguapés,[4] scraped from the sheaths of the banks by the curved, sharp sword of the torrent.

On the first of November of that year, the Amazon began to fulfil its ritual obligation to slowly flood the land, as always, with the throbbing of an exhausted heartbeat. The first to be threatened were the cornfields, beans and watermelons in the lowland areas. Later, the cacao, orange and manioc trees of the floodplains would be devastated. The *terra firma* loomed above this cataclysm, looking on indifferently at the wreckage caused by the swell.

On top of that spine of higher land there was a humble and inconspicuous cemetery, inaccessible to the haughty flood. Beneath tufts of tall grass, the opulent fronds of a mango tree and the stunted growth of some guava trees, people had been sleeping in this 'terra preta'[5] for over a hundred years. Only about a dozen wooden crosses could be seen. These had begun to rot as soon as the funeral was over, and yet others were planted in freshly-dug graves. These would then disappear in their turn, but new ones were on the way. The ones that were currently there were merely the latest ones to have been planted....

The cemetery usually lay under dense brush and sprawling grasses. Pigs roamed around, grunting. Other animals grazed quietly, lounging around on top of the unmarked graves. On All Soul's Day, however, it was tended to by villagers from the surrounding area, who would arrive to piously decorate the abandoned site. Early in the morning, they weeded plots of grass and picked up fallen crosses. By the time afternoon came, a freshly trimmed field was awaiting its pilgrims.

---

4. A family of aquatic plants, with submerged, free-floating and emergent varieties (*Pontederiacea*).

5. Literally 'black soil', this is a type of man-made soil found in the Amazon basin. It was made by adding a mixture of human remains, broken pottery and charcoal to the largely infertile soil of the flood plains. Here, the graveyard itself is intended.

As night fell, montarias made their way to the shore of the cemetery from all sides, heading along the ideal ribs of an immense open fan. Soon the cemetery was overflowing with people, almost all of them dressed up for a joyous open-air party.

Countless candles were burning on the ground; and the tiny votive flames gave the impression of throbbing golden flowers blossoming suddenly on the grass. Some musicians, grouped in a corner, were playing instruments in a sort of funeral march. Girls and boys swarmed among these little magical, floral lights. They were irresistibly animated, scarcely unable to contain their laughter despite the toccata and the mortuary solemnity, which seemed to affect only the elderly.

Gabriel was there with his whole family, even his little grandchildren.

Around ten o'clock, the throng of visitors left the wild campo santo and gathered at the hut of old Agostinho and his pajé[6] sister, in the mangrove forest, to dance for the rest of the night.

Gabriel, however, headed home in the other direction. He was not in the mood for merrymaking. A few days earlier, he had learnt that Colonel Roberto was insisting on taking his land, and since then the old caboclo had felt disgusted with everything.

The boss of the entire coastal plain, and the biggest political influence in the Municipality, Roberto was also the region's ultimate plunderer. Only the tuxaua prospered while everything else fell into backwardness and misery. He had made his start in cavalier fashion by appropriating Calixto's little place and establishing a wood port[7] there. That was enough...and after about twelve years, what he had initially acquired grew, spreading little by little like an untreatable leprosy spreads from one spot on the skin to the entire body. Thus he ended up taking possession of all the places around him, and with them unrivalled wealth and prestige.

As a result of an unfortunate retrogressive tendency, the regime of small property was being devoured by that of large-scale ownership.

---

6. A word that is Old Tupi in origin: an indigenous healer or shaman figure.

7. A place on the riverbank where the steamer pulls up or docks to receive firewood and drop off passengers.

The insatiable politician was one of the factors in this criminal economic misappropriation, whether by money, deceit or force of violence. So much so that a single individual soul, overpowered by evil instincts, even acting within the limited field of its own influence, can disturb the proper evolutionary development of an entire society. Affluence and dominance is correlated not with the 'great man' but with his inverse, the social mushroom.

In the area that this bigshot had ravaged, only one nook had escaped his rapacious hand. It was the little spot occupied for over forty years by Gabriel, who had received it from his father, who was also called Gabriel. The place still preserved the same ranch of cocoa trees, bacabas,[8] abius, açaís and orange trees from Gabriel's father's time. The son still remembered seeing him, under that same grove of trees, squatting down, perched over a taquari[9] and calmly watching the passing batelões, igarités, montarias, rafts, and balsas....

The Colonel was annoyed by that strip of land wedged awkwardly into his vast rural estate. He was resolved not to tolerate anything that encroached on his property. And why should a petty little cabo-clo stand in his way, resisting the generous offers he had made? For something of no real value, he had risked spending a couple of million reis! He had friends in Manaus and was hoping to get everything sorted without too much bother.

Poor Gabriel knew very well that his small farm was not worth anything: it was a mud hut isolated in a small várzea. But it meant everything to him, because if he were to sell it on for a few pennies, where would he go with his huge family: two widowed daughters and three unmarried sisters-in-law, plus a bunch of curumins? Any empty land he could get around there would be completely sunken, rendered useless if there was any flooding....

He was convinced, therefore, that he should hold on to his native territory; moreover, usucaption was enshrined in law, recognising and

---

8. A fruiting palm tree (*Oenocarpus bacaba*).

9. (*Mabea angustifolia*.)

guaranteeing his right to possess this land, which he had maintained peacefully and quietly for more than forty years now.

It was not, therefore, some stupid whim on Gabriel's part, this unwillingness to part with what he thought belonged to him. What is more, it resulted from his natural and immanent attachment to the land where he was born, along with his family situation, which placed him in a position of responsibility.

Roberto's attitude, meanwhile, was essentially one of cruelty and spite. That despicable old caboclo was an embarrassment to his hitherto triumphant passion for domination. So the chief could not rest until, finally, he made up his mind to strike.

After insistent repeated offers to buy his property, Gabriel felt that the time had come for the final battle in defence of it. He had seen how similar disputes had ended up. In the face of the political boss, there was ultimately nobody who did not back down. No one had ever been able to avoid surrendering up these properties that he had his eye on and lusted after greedily.

But Gabriel did not lose heart, trusting in God's justice. That is why he was going to carry on until the end. A certain assurance took hold of him. He went on working, even though he was still apprehensive.

Faced with the obstinacy of this caboclo, the Colonel finally decided to take the matter in hand. He had done his duty, sending word about the purchase to Gabriel many times. Gabriel had stubbornly refused to give in. But there was no way that he—a brave, fabulously wealthy leader with a short fuse—would give up on ousting his rival.

Moreover, people everywhere were eagerly awaiting the result of the feud between the 'big' and the 'small'. Not just out of a malign curiosity, but because popular opinion, since the Gospels, has always had sympathy for the weak and the persecuted. For Roberto it was a question of self-respect, for he had heard that the caboclo had invoked 'lawses'[10] and that he would neither give away nor sell the land he occupied. Very well, he would petition the Government for it. Let the caboclo protest. He was in cloud-cuckoo land....

---

10. In caboclo vernacular: '*lezes*' rather than standard Brazilian Portuguese '*leis*'.

One day, the luckless Gabriel had gone to harpoon a pirarucu and to shoot tambaquis[11] and turtles in the lake. He had diligently equipped his montaria for this purpose. He had not forgotten a thing. A sarará,[12] an arrow made from a stalk, the pracuúba stick, the harpoon rope, the harpoon itself his wooden float, the gourd of water flour, a piece of ground pirapitinga, the basket containing catauaris and the ponga[13] with which the fisherman whips the water to attract the gluttonous fish, who are listening out for appetising fruits such as the caimbé, the abiurana, and the tarumã to fall....

During his absence an engineer appeared, accompanied by Roberto's henchmen, at one end of the caboclo's plot. They did not stay for long. In two short hours they finished their work, sighting some directions and measuring some lines, to the astonishment of Gabriel's women and children, who looked on suspicious and mute.

Upon returning from fishing, he learnt that the engineer had been 'correcting' his land. The wretched old man went completely mad. He spent hours in a distracted state out in the yard. Nearby there had been a high abiu tree where a surucuá bird used to perch and emit the same short song, repeating its own name: 'surucuá, surucuá'.

These days there was very little left of the tree, because an apuizeiro was squeezing it, leeching from it, swallowing it up in a prolonged but persistent and all-consuming relationship.

---

11. A large species of freshwater fish (*Colossoma macropomum*).

12. Since there was discord among contemporary critics on this term, it is possible this was a misprint or misunderstanding on the part of Rangel. José Verissimo claimed it was something to do with the Tupi verb *sará*, to unroll. Quintino Cunha believed it was a special type of arrow used in fishing. It is also the name of a reddish-winged ant that swarms in the light on sunny days after the rains.

13. In *A Pesca na Amazónia* (Rio de Janeiro: Livraria clássica de Alves, 1895), José Verissimo suggests that the name of this tool, which is used to beat the surface of the water, refers to the sound made by falling fruit, which it is meant to imitate (103–4).

The apuizeiro[14] is an octopus in plant form. It wraps itself around its sacrifice, extending thousands of tentacles over it. Gilliat's octopus[15] had eight arms and four hundred suckers; those of the apuizeiro are uncountable. In the structure of its tissue, every one of its microscopic cells takes the form of a thirsty mouth. And the whole struggle takes place silently, without a whisper. It begins by curling around the branch, which is attacked by woody threads, coming from who knows where. Then these threads swell, and, once swollen, begin to proliferate into others still. Finally, the weft thickens and advances slowly, in order to mesh together with its prey, which it completely replaces. The apuizeiro is like a shroud enwrapping a corpse: the corpse rots but the shroud lives on, immortal.

The abiu tree would have only a short time left to live. A desperate effort could be sensed in the miserable creature, determined as it was to break free from the noose in which it was held. Yet its captor seemed to become stronger, gripping this unfortunate organism that was being strangled by the gradual, unexpected pressure with each and every one of its constricting fibres. The process was irreversible. With a machete, the tentacles could be torn to shreds and ripped out. But it would be enough if just a small piece of capillary filament was left stuck to the tree. This would allow the executioner to reattach itself to its victim, who would have no chance of survival. The polyp is part of a colony of polyps. Generations live in a single body, in a single part, in a single fragment. Every part, no matter how small, is alive. It cannot be reduced to an individual. It is the solidarity of the infinitesimal, essential, elemental, inseparable and indivisible in the republic of synergetic embryos. What remains is always enough to bring it back to life. It reproduces easily, in its latent but irrepressible haste to procreate more and more.

---

14. Also known as a matapau tree in Brazil, this refers to a strangler fig, which encompasses various species in the *Ficus* genus. The 'strangling' growth habit is an evolutionary adaption to environments where light is scarce. The plants steal nutrients from their victims, eventually killing them.

15. A reference to the famous scene in Victor Hugo's 1866 *Toilers of the Sea*.

The abiu tree's canopy of small leathery and glabrous leaves had almost disappeared into the broad foliage of the monstrous parasite.

In fact, this duel between forms of plant life represented a perfectly human spectacle. Roberto, the potentate, was himself a social apuizeiro.

Interrupting this schism, Gabriel's affectionate grandchildren surrounded him hoping for embraces which did not come. They were surprised to see their grandfather's eyes welling up with elusive tears. Gabriel never smiled again. An infinite grief was spreading through every fibre of his soul. He trembled with anger; his heart seemed fit to burst. He then felt a horrible sensation as though he were suffocating, as if he were being carried away by a spiralling whirlwind....

Compadre Raimundo and his other neighbours tried to calm him down. Compadre Zacarias had even offered to get the protest into a newspaper. But it was all to no avail. The usurper's heavy foot would crush him like all the others. Poor people were not able to keep hold of their possessions when rich men were around. Gabriel would be in no position to resist to this absorption by the White man. What belonged to him would end up in the hands of this potentate whose gargantuan appetite was ravaging that peaceful coast like a swarm of vandals.

The caboclo and his companions foresaw this fate. What were they but humble creatures sure to be defeated in this fight against a stronger mob? Before, the land was large, people were few, and they were content with little. Then the Cearense arrived in tumultuous waves of occupation. Land became more scarce with the increasing number of outsiders—people who, even worse, who had arrived with the exclusive aim of making a fast buck.

So it was that the human drama began to unfold on the Amazonian stage, creating situations peculiar to such an environment. The staggering immigrant population was like a Medusa's head; their ambitious interests immediately clashed with those of the natives. So many were coming where there had previously been so few: there was latent opposition. The fact is that they were determined to do anything. They were driven by an ardent, fiery impulse. Unfathomable miseries impelled them to fight, while the caboclo, mouldering in a

Capua[16] of pristine waters and fertile land, could not withstand the onslaught of these legions that came bearing hunger.

Colonel Roberto, from wíba, had risen to General from a simple soldier who had started off in that historic invasion of the Amazon—a modern Anabasis.[17] He had deservedly earned his stripes, his soul even more audacious than those of the audacious mass from which he emerged.

Gabriel wondered why this man wanted so much land. It certainly wasn't to cultivate it, because apart from a few low spots in Caniço, where a herd of cattle from Rio Branco was grazing, everything was unusable bush or scrubland. It would appear that, by this indirect means, he was enjoying a certain pride in 'putting an end to the caboclos'. At this thought Gabriel felt stirred; he saw a heroic path before him, and his strength returned to him. Revolted, he silently resolved to make a solemn demonstration of his resistance to the mighty Roberto.

After a few months, the caboclo was summoned to leave the hut because the Colonel had already been granted the coveted definitive title to the property, with all the attendant rubrics, seals, stamps, and registry entries. Resolution had already matured in the expelled man's conscience. The new owner of the little farm, a merciful intruder, granted him a fortnight at the latest to get out. But Gabriel would not move an inch. He would have to be pulled out of that ravine by the roots, like a bush. It was the place where his eyes had opened for the first time, and where his ancestors had been laid to rest.

As the final deadline approached, the caboclo left the house, saying he was going to look for a high sandbank where he could settle down with his 'people'.

---

16. A reference to the city in Italy, which was said to the most opulent and pleasant in the land. Hannibal famously seized the city and made his winter quarters there. His enjoyment of the delights on offer brought disaster to his campaign against Rome.

17. A reference to that work of the same by Xenophon. It describes a Greek campaign in Persia. The term is particularly apt: *anabasis* refers to a journey to the interior of a country.

It so happened, however, that on the day Roberto had decreed for the eviction of the 'squatter', the family, desolate and in tears, waited for old Gabriel to no avail. He had not returned. Helpful neighbours plunged into the forest in search of the caboclo and scoured the river, searching upstream and downstream, conjecturing that *perhaps his boat had capsized?*

The missing man's wives and children, a brood banished from the nest by a rude barbarian, took shelter in the house of compadre Raimundo.

Later, Gabriel was found. He was in the old capoeira scrubland that covered a stretch of his besieged little farm. Covered by the huge trunk of a sapucaia tree[18] and disguised by lush anajás[19] branches, the caboclo lay buried up to his chest. His skull protruded horrifically from the churned earth, putrescent, hanging off the exposed cervical vertebrae. Beneath the azure cloth of his jacket, draped from his detached shoulder blades, his bare arms could be seen. His thorax had already been eaten away by worms, all the rotting muscle lining having been stripped away in an ignoble deliquescence. His hands were crumpled, the phalanges hideously embedded in the clay left over from filling the grave.

In his last moments alive, Gabriel had arranged himself like this in a final evocative gesture, that of a miser caught by surprise and securing his treasure. Having buried himself in the tragic absurdity of his madness, he would remain in his own soil forever. When omnipotent Wealth, in conjunction with Pride and Ambition, came to tear him away from his family stronghold, he had decided upon this unprecedented and macabre protest: a grave in which would be buried alive the very man who had dug it.

So it was that the caboclo, shut out from the bosom of his beloved land, was ferociously welcomed back into that same bosom. Unable to live on in the land of his birth, he made it his tomb. As heroic as

18. The cream nut or monkey pot, a tree in the Brazil nut family *Lecythidaceae* (*Lecythis Pisonis*).

19. A variety of palm (*Attalea concina*).

Prometheus unbound, he had ploughed himself into the earth like an armadillo.

The iniquity visited upon him well deserved this frightful lesson. Let the haughty conqueror halo himself in triumph as he might; in treading upon this land, now made the sacred asylum of a dead man, he would be violating it with the insolence of a sacrilegious plunderer.

8. The Tenacity of Life

You will taste death, O flower, with delight.

Jean Moréas, 'Les Stances'

The silver half-ring of a new moon was almost lost in the seamless, heavy quilt of an intensely black sky. In a display of opulent, high-class mourning, some strange undertaker had hurriedly laid out all of their best crepe and black velvet on the circle of the horizon.

Immersed in this darkness, as if at the bottom of a reservoir, surrounded by craggy cliffs, I drifted in the dark current, which propelled and guided the 'Viola', the water itself imperceptibly dragging the montaria along with it. The helmsman kept a watchful eye on our placid passage through this cavern of night.

In the thick shadows one could discern the dim banks of the igarapé, because they sparkled with the fantastic fire of fireflies, like precious jewels set out in the shop window display of the slate riverbanks. In streaks of twinkling stars, in leaps of forge sparks, in splashes of fiery rain, in a sprinkle of bright flashes, the lights swirled in the air like the lights of a suburb or luminous flour sifted and scattered by an invisible sieve.

Innumerable little lamps shone out—the usual aerial devotees taking part in the Fogaréu Procession[1] or celebrating Our Lady of Light.[2]

---

1. A traditional Catholic procession held annually in some cities in Brazil and Portugal (famously Braga) during Holy Week. During the procession, dozens of farricocos—hooded, barefoot men representing Roman soldiers—walk through the streets holding torches.

2. Nossa Senhora das Candeias: a title by which the Catholic church venerates the Virgin Mary. The tradition emerged in the Canary Islands but is particularly strong in Portugal and Brazil.

Far and wide a battle seemed to be raging. Shots rang out everywhere. Ever since the feral night had swept over the landscape with its vastness and gloom, an extraordinary fusillade had erupted along the banks. So much so that the fireflies looked like the embers of a burning bamboo grove....

Sometimes the shooting stopped, only to restart later, yet more insistent and intense, a line of fire in advance of combat. The rifles were unloaded in a frenzied volley until their magazines were exhausted, or blocked by misfires.

There is no rubber tapper, so to speak, who does not own a rifle: the Winchester rifle. It is the means of ensuring subsistence and also the enforcer of the Law. Everywhere this is assured by force, which, by Carlyle's account, *is* the Law.[3] 'Here, justice is 44', the rubber tapper proclaims, alluding to the calibre of the weapon that defends him in the wilderness. This is a literal translation of the concept that von Ihering[4] formulated, less crudely but based on the same philosophy, summing up the sad living conditions in these societies.

Each bullet cost, at the very least, half a penny. So that, on top of the cost of the detonations, a fortune was being scattered through the mouths of these guns, going up in smoke, flashes, and rumbling echoes.

It was the eve of St. John's Day. The rubber tappers were happy to commemorate the Saint in this loud and profligate manner. Not having access to fireworks, they set off their rifles, firing thousands of bullets which hissed through the air, flying past one another ineffectually. Like this they would waste what they actually needed the next day for hunting, in a traditional celebration which involved shooting the innocent darkness.

---

3. Thomas Carlyle, Scottish essayist and historian—presumably this is Rangel's interpretation of his metaphysics of force, and perhaps a reference to his *On Heroes, Hero-Worship, and the Heroic in History.*

4. Rudolf von Ihering, German jurist and legal scholar, best known for his 1872 *Der Kampf ums Recht (The Struggle for Law).*

Even when a great wave of light spread out softly in space from the east, the firefight continued with great intensity, shattering the silence of those plains with its extraordinary uproar.

After the sun had risen, and I had passed through a flock of buritis,[5] periquiteiras,[6] and taxizeiros,[7] the flowers of which were already rust coloured, I suddenly came across some roofs made from jarina.[8] This was where I was headed, at Cambito's request, to hire someone to do a job.

Drawing closer, the little patch of beach was clearly visible, and I had the 'Viola' pulled over onto it. We were immediately greeted on the sandy ramp by a flight of yellow butterflies, which began to flutter in the air like a handful of autumn leaves raised by a whirling gust of wind.

Disembarking, I climbed the hillside. A huge ramshackle barracão sat gravely beside a gleaming sugar cane plantation. Right at the foot of the steps, in front of the door, a lemon tree was bursting with new shoots, weighed down by the burden of its sulphur-yellow fruit.

Cambito wasn't there, the housekeeper told me, he had gone to the lake to shoot some fish. But he shouldn't be long. And as soon as he said this, the boss came back with his catch. He was carrying a basket full of maparás, curimatãs and jundiás, and had the rifle that he had been using to shoot the fish slung over his shoulder. The Cearense realised we were there, and graciously extended his calloused hand to me, after giving the basket to the housekeeper.

At the host's invitation to go upstairs and sit down, waiting for him to return, I sat down on a bench in the corner of a room surrounded on both sides by a balcony. I gazed at the surrounding landscape,

---

5. A palm tree which produces the 'moriche' palm fruit. Alexander von Humboldt was famously impressed by the degree to which it was interconnected with the rest of the environment. (*Mauritia flexuosa.*)

6. A tree with yellow flowers and a number of medicinal uses (*Cochlospermum orinocense*).

7. A tree with deep red flowers that resemble hydrangeas. They colour the banks of the Lower Amazon profusely in July and August. (*Triplaris americana.*)

8. A dioecious palm (*Phytelephas macrocarpa*).

chrome-plated in the splendour of the quiet morning. Emerging from the inner rooms of the barracão, where the screams and cries of a child seemed to go on and on, Cambito promptly came to settle me down in a small room whose only window opened onto a view of light green reeds.

Ten interminable days I stayed in this dreadful house, which stood frowning on the edge of the long, deep gorge of the desolate igarapé. Cambito lived there along with his wife and a daughter. He had a haggard disposition, with dull and vacant eyes in an oppilated face, but the gentle smile and soft speech of a calm man. The woman was tall and corpulent, with a fresh and sanguine countenance, bursting with the warm colours and opulent lines of a Rubens naiad, in those remote confines of the kingdom of endemic beriberi[9] and malaria.

But the daughter was a morose, emaciated figure, the very idealisation of Suffering straight out of the artist's mould. She had come into the world blind, deaf-mute, paraplegic, and insane to boot. Upon being born she had opened her eyes to life, but found it as opaque as the womb whence she came. Yet her pupils were of a velvety hue, resembling two black haematites, rolling inertly under the faint parchment of her eyelids.

Infantile encephalitis had struck this timid creature, who flailed about in fits of chorea which made her little arms convulse and her torso twist and shake, as if her entire being were conspiring to cast her outward into space....

Day and night, the little girl would not rest. She struggled continually, she cried ceaselessly, as if the tender dough of her sensitive flesh were being torn to shreds by invisible sackcloth. I was struck by the spectacle of this unprecedented martyrdom. Her camellia body was constantly quivering; cries rang out through her red lips; her little wax hands retracted and stretched out as her thin arms shook nervously.

And there was no remedy for this congenital malady. None! The fate of that girl was atrocious, with no light of reason, no light in her eyes; half stone, half nerves.

---

9. A disease found largely in the tropics caused by a vitamin B1 deficiency.

And so it had been for more than five years now, minute by minute, the tenacity of life maintaining the higher, cerebrospinal disorder by way of the lower phenomena of idiot vegetable existence. To think that life persisted in its tenacity within this alienated infanta,[10] while in the surrounding region many a sturdy cowboy had been finished off by a fatal chill or a cunning swamp! One might say that this debilitated little being had received all at once her bill for all the evils that were supposed to befall her later on in life; and, thus arraigned, she was to be spared any more blows, having been given so much to suffer in one go.

This suffering no longer rattled anyone; it was in the natural order of things. Although everyone there should have been tormented by this spectacle, revolted by its injustice, it did not disturb or move them any more. The little girl's crying prevented me from sleeping; it caused me devastating and irrepressible anxiety. Its painful reverberations reached my hammock to chase off my sleep. They seared my soul at every moment, unnerving me.

Whenever my heart felt most overwhelmed by bitterness, I would flee the barracão, wandering into the sugar cane field and gloomily retiring into the mill that grinds the cane at its annual first growth.

The apparatus, constructed out of Itaúba wood, was installed in a vast barn. It was set in motion by two men who, enclosed in an immense wheel, began to walk in the same direction inside it. This caused it to turn because they were breaking the balance of the system with their strides. This was the work of the *tread mill*.[11] The grinders bit into the bundles of cane, creaking as they crushed them, and the garapa flowed in great gouts into a vat nearby. The tired men, crammed in and hunched over, tried to climb to the top of the wheel, but this only brought them back to the same point from which they started. The exertion left them bathed in sweat, prostrate with fatigue. The milling ceased; the molasses boiled in the pots; an alembic distilled the brandy....

---

10. A daughter of a king of Portugal; a princess.

11. In English in the original.

As it was getting late and mealtime was approaching, I had to return to the barracão, where the delirious little invalid would be waiting for me. No one else was worried or bothered. People came and went, and indifference of habit meant that they no longer paid any attention to her torment. Business was discussed, incidents were commented on, jokes were laughed at, and constantly, in the background, the piercing screams of the innocent girl, sweeping across the walls of the house, infiltrating them with her accursed suffering.... In the numb stillness of the night, that cry seemed even more pronounced. There was nothing to stop it. The whole barracão seemed to be gasping in anguish at the child's torture, but it was only the wind moaning through the cracks.... The sunlight seeped through the gaps in the walls and roof at the sounds of the morning, but even then, the terror did not dissipate....

One day, Cambito confessed to me that he wanted his daughter to die. This would put an end to the ordeal. His wife, Doca, did not want it, he said. She was resigned to it. If God had sent her daughter into the world like this, then he would call her back when it suited him—that was her opinion. The husband would then sink into thought, lost in sombre brooding, repeating the phrase: 'If God sent my daughter into the world like this....'

'Tomorrow, little Maria will be six years old,' he announced to me, moved by emotion. 'Another year, you see, what a fate! But we're used to it now....' And he left me in order to go and greet a cauchero who had just arrived.

D. Bustamante was wearing a white dolman suit. His attire was so prim it would have been appropriate for a nobleman's stroll along the paths of a summer garden. The gentleman was travelling in a convoy of ubás,[12] full of his Sipibo and Conibo Indians,[13] men and women

---

12. A type of canoe constructed from the bark of an entire tree or a single hollowed-out trunk.

13. Two indigenous tribes from Peru. They have since merged into a single tribe known as the Shipibo-Conibo people.

striped with jenipapo, half-naked, wrapped in cushmas;[14] an Adonis come to preside over the ranch of these colourful, ragtag demons.

They had all come from a tambo[15] on the Pischis,[16] on an obscure but epic march down the Paquiteia to the Ucayali, up the Abuaua, then the Mateus, then the Pacaí, and on from the Oromano, through a sweep of water, to the igarapé that had brought them here, in search of the riches embedded in the bark of the casteloas.

The cauchero is a vagrant prowler; a sinister jequitiranaboia,[17] he walks through the woods stalking and killing whatever tree he is drawn to. I had heard them referred to with barely concealed hatred. Everyone stigmatised them, summing them up with a nickname: 'wretched gringos'. A confused and conflicting historical racial feud was further souring owing to the rivalry between men involved in the same trade. In a society becoming sedentary, the nomad was frowned upon. The only thing missing was the warning message that can still be read today at the edge of villages in France: *Défense aux nomades de stationner.*[18]

No one had much time for the caucheros, these apostates resigned and restricted to destruction. And yet they were astonishingly courageous. The campaign *en el monte, en la montaña* was worthy of an epic. They were not audacious settlers. The conquest was hastened by them. They were a vanguard party, explorers, skirting the enemy mass of the hinterland in the north-western frontier of the country

---

14. A type of long cloak, often painted.

15. From the Quechua *tampu*, 'inn'. In this context it refers to something like the barracão (from these regions to the north and west of the Amazon), a rural communal house.

16. One of the sources of the Pachitea River in Peru, itself a source of the Ucayali.

17. The lantern fly or peanut bug, a planthopper insect. From Tupi *iakirána*, 'cicada' and *mboia* 'snake'.

18. 'Nomads prohibited from stopping here'. An artefact of the French 1912 law on the movement of 'nomads', here meaning Roma people, which remained in force for more than sixty years.

from the rear, in successive guerrilla raids. These filibusters[19] got ahead of the seringueiro and even surprised him with the news that he could advance....

However, here was D. Bustamante, who had come to negotiate with Cambito about felling the timber that flourished on land occupied by the Cearense man.

When the caucheros were initially making their adventurous raid through the uninhabited region, they did not have to ask for anything; but after the army of seringueiros camped out and took over the discovered land, the whole forest was divided up by landowners. It is interesting that, on maps from Bolivia and Peru, this land appears to be trapped in a cartoonish curve, indicating the intrusion of Brazil's territory in revoked and out-of-date pacts. This conventional graphical boundary, which the centuries-old claims of two foreign governments had watermarked, printed, and circulated around the world, was shattered by the hatchets[20] of our countrymen, keeping national sovereignty in the balance. Despite the disdain of the Castilian[21] cartographers, the cauchero could not then take another step without permission. The worker bees of the seringa repelled the caucho drones. In fact, the infinite circle in which the feverish cauchero wandered so ambitiously had suddenly narrowed. Their political fictions and diplomatic intrigues had been undone by the arrival of the people from Ceará. Now, trapped in the clutches of this latifundium,[22] the cauchero's role as free explorer of the sertão had been transmuted into that of a stoic hard-working pauper.

D. Bustamante could not agree on the price Cambito demanded. He simply accepted a cup of coffee, and, resigned and humourless,

---

19. In Portuguese, 'flibusteiro' refers in particular to pirates in the Antilles Sea during the seventeenth and eighteenth centuries.

20. Specifically, the long-handled machadinhos of the seringueiros, their primary instrument. The men themselves were sometimes even called machadinhos owing to their reliance on these tools.

21. I.e. Spanish-speaking; in this context, Peruvian or Bolivian.

22. A large agricultural estate operating within a slave economy.

the Peruvian went back to the ubás, which soon descended through the sandbanks that the igarapé was piling up on its empty, boulder-strewn riverbed.

No sooner had the savages and their gallant captain disappeared than another man, hot on his heels, arrived at the hut, in pensive mood. It was the Portuguese Tomé Rodrigues Pereira, a labourer on a road in the Cambito rubber plantation.

By virtue of what arts had this man from Minho come to the Upper Amazon, an unusual addition to the national forces that occupied and dominated those lands? For they were Brazilian and Northern legions, the ones that advanced toward the north of Brazil. Foreigners stayed in Manaus, amidst the cruelty of commerce, the bill of trade and its discount, the artifice of exchange. In having undertaken this fantastic enterprise of entering and settling in such a dangerous region, our compatriot was quite the daredevil. Eager but cautious foreigners tended to stop at a strategic point favourable to speculative trading. The native simply sacrificed himself, heading for strange parts where Death had a throne and his vassals; the European emigrant wasn't going to risk his skin for next to nothing....

But the Lusitanian was there all right. Although his frame was as strong as that of Hercules, one of his legs was half-devoured by a wound that had gone bad. At first it had been a small red rash, reminiscent of an ecthyma pustule; then it had grown and spread, resistant to all drying powders and disinfectants, pine nut milk, iodine—everything that had been recommended and considered effective. From the knee to the malleolus, the deep sore had corroded the tissues, and was about to leave the extremity of the tibia visible.

Many people living in these remote outposts were affected by such lesions of inexplicable cause. The application of a hot iron was an anaplerotic[23] to which the affliction showed no resistance. While homemade plasters or iodoform, boric acid or sublimates were of no use, these cankers would yield to the violence of thermocauterisation.

---

23. A remedy which attempts to granulate the site of a wound or ulcer.

Informing me as to the origin and course of his illness, the unfortunate man told me about his life. He had never again returned to his birthplace. 'Twenty years, sir, for this world of Christ....' From the village in Minho located on a pleasant slope of vineyards and pines, he had come to be a ship's mate in Funchal; then, in Bragança, in Pará, he had opened a grocer's shop. He did not even know why he was there, in the rubber plantation, in the stupor of this illness. He had never again heard from homeland or family—that is, his homestead and his fiancée, which was all he had. And he was wholly unable to send a letter over there in his own handwriting, to speak of what was in his soul: his longing for the land and the love of his wife! Attributing his whole misfortune to the original sin of not knowing how to read and write, he deplored his illiteracy. He was envious of what culture I had. 'To know how to read and write! A beautiful gift! A beautiful gift!' he monologued, sighing. The poor fellow had not worked for a year. As his muscles wore out, God knows, his accumulated earnings also vanished!

'I'm sure I'll stay here, if the Virgin doesn't come to rescue me', stammered Tomé, glancing down at the S-belt from the front gully. 'The boss wants to convince me that this is nothing, that it'll heal with the fire. We'll see! But there's no getting away from the fact that this bloody disease is going to kick my arse....'

Cambito decided to let the Galician[24] rest and to apply the intense treatment to him the next day. The Portuguese had resigned himself to this, agreeing *in extremis*.

That night, the eve of the little madwoman's birthday, I was stricken with insomnia. I opened the bedroom window and was immediately invaded by the contrast of quiet nature, hypnotised by the pearly dew in the moonlight, which was bathing the barracão where that little creature cried continuously. The rough leaves of the canaria reeds took on a pewter lustre. A complete, soporific peace lulled all things into a deep sleep, in the chaste, milky light of the moon. The stars

---

24. Although nominally in today's Portugal, the area covered by former province of Minho shares many cultural traits with Galicia.

were studded in the sky and, like an ethereal garment, the foulard of the nebulae unfurled foamily upon the décolleté of the night.

Only the child, lying nearby, did not rest, as if she were being barbarically tortured by a secret relentless executioner.

Friezes of golden spikelets were announcing the dawn as the brightness of the stars faded by the time I closed the window, falling back into the hammock, overcome by sleep.

I woke up very late, at the invitation to attend the treatment of the nasty wound. I went down the steps to the lemon tree, finding the patient on the table, a group of six people surrounding him in preparation. One of them patiently built the clay border around the ulcer to restrict the field of application of the heat during the topical cauterisation. Then they held the 'sailor'[25] by the arms, legs, and torso. Another went to fetch a tin of simmering American lard that was hanging from the tripod above a chip fire. In one swift movement, the man poured the burning liquid onto the dreadful wound. After the hissing, smoke rose from the putrid, boiled tissue. The victim screamed and tried to squirm away. The smell of burning flesh marked the end of the savage operation. Once this was done, they took the collapsed Tomé to the room where he was being put up in the barracão.

A little while later, while we were having lunch, Cambito was informed that the patient had just died. Beside the lunch table, on the lap of the Rubenesque Doca, the little blind girl, wriggling frantically, was voraciously gobbling a plate of porridge.

The incredible capriciousness of life! It had quit the body of the strong but would not give up this fragile, weak little creature who had just turned six! To celebrate her birthday, her mother had dressed her in a new, lacy nightgown with blue silk bows. In a twist of irony, the little monster's face glowed with the rosy colour of healthy babies.

When I went back down the igarapé from Cambito's shack, the small stream had become a deep and voluminous current. The water had risen overnight and was now a torrent. All it took was one day's rain. The stream was overflowing. It would not be long, however,

---

25. A derogatory term for the Portuguese used in certain parts of northern Brazil.

before it drained away and once again revealed the sandbars that scarred its bed.

A few beaches further on, I came across the bivouacked Peruvians. Around bonfires, naked women were butchering monkeys, plucking macaws. These 'red slaves' followed my canoe with their eyes as it passed. Mr D. Bustamante, looking just as dapper as before, raised his Chilean hat solemnly and soberly, greeting me courteously.

From far downstream, the agonising cry of the mad child continued to plague me, tearing me apart even from so far away. Then a thought flashed into my brain: *And yet, all it would take is a drop of poison or a scalpel blade, in the hands of a merciful person, to put an end to the tenacity of life....*

9. Maibi

It is a wild and desert place.
Might it be cursed? I seem to see
On the crippled roots of yonder
Tree a crimson smear of blood.

Heinrich Heine, Atta Troll

A tall, brutish figure, his mouth masked by the fringe of his bushy moustache, said to another haggard individual ravaged by malaria and malnutrition, with a few stiff hairs at the corners of his lips and on his protruding chin, 'So, the deal is done...we understand each other, right? You no longer owe me anything and you have to leave Maibi with Sergio.'

'Yes sir', replied the scrawny man, holding back a sob.

This dialogue was taking place at the counter in the warehouse between Lieutenant Marciano, owner of the Soledade, and one of his customers, Sabino da Maibi. By the time the hideous transaction between the two men was over and done with, the sun was descending, biting into the green-black frieze of the forest, and the light from outside filtered into the barracão through the gaps in the ill-fitting paxiúba boards as if it were straining through the iron bars of a dungeon in which two reprobates were confined.

What deal had finally been struck? Sabino owed his boss seven contos[1] and two hundred réis, which would have taken him four years

---

1. A conto, literally 'a count of réis', was one million réis. The real was introduced to Brazil by Dutch and Portuguese colonists in the seventeenth century, and was untethered from the Portuguese real by 1750. The First Brazilian Republic (1889–1930) saw rapid inflation of the currency, so that by the final years of the Republic the conto had become the practical unit of currency.

at least to pay off. So he had sold off his wife to another customer of the rubber plantation, Sergio, who would in exchange take on the responsibility of paying off his debt. The most common of commercial arrangements: a transfer of debt, with the assent of the creditor, in order to settle the books.

The exchange was in the boss's interest, as he could be more confident in Sergio, a young man renowned as a hard worker. And Sabino would work more enthusiastically now that he could hope to actually make a profit at the end of the year. Along with his wife, his greatest burden had also disappeared: the seven-and-a-bit contos. Just the thought of the debt had been enough to throw him into a deplorable state of despondency. Sabino had understood that, with his wife in tow, no matter how hard he worked, he would never pay off the ever-increasing arrears, and would become a slave. That debt had been a pair of iron shackles.

Paying off the 'balance' is the obsession of the rubber plantation worker.[2] And how can this not be so, since the 'balance' is freedom? The rubber industry's regime has been abominable. White slavery was instituted for labour! A specific feature of the nation's cultural development, it was brought about by the demands of lawless profiteering. The system emerged from the contingencies of the struggle. Not by order of some authority—there was none—but through tacit agreement among all. Besides, what needed to be organised, in the middle of the jungle, was something that the country's social and political opinion makers, centred in the rua do Ouvidor,[3] had never even imagined. It was said to be a nation of bandits, a Land of Cockaigne; no one ever thought it necessary to provide any supervision of labour—as

---

2. The 'balance', the carta de saldo, is in fact the document the rubber tapper receives at the barracão when he settles his bills. For an account of the debt entrapment faced by the seringueiro, see da Cunha, 'General Impression', *Amazon*, 14–17.

3. The street in Rio de Janeiro where all the major newspapers were based up until the turn of the twentieth century, and therefore a synonym for the news media.

if it were nobody's business. Incredible as it may seem, it was rubber tappers who struck a blow against the founding law of a free nation! Because, under the very specific conditions that prevailed at that time, it turned out that just relying on what happened spontaneously was not enough. After all, a rubber plantation is not a cattle ranch, a coffee plantation, or a sugar cane mill. What sufficed for the Rio Grande campaign, west of São Paulo, in the interior of Pernambuco, was not sufficient on the banks of the Madeira, the Purus, and the Juruá. What the legislation didn't provide for, the nascent industry would handle itself. It wasn't straight-out cruelty, but the result of Capital protecting its own interests. All quite logical, or at least inevitable. The statutes of this new society striving to establish itself adopted this as their basic principle: the seringueiro could not leave the rubber plantation without settling accounts with the employer.

That is why, on many occasions, Sabino had felt the impulse to throw down the rubber milk bucket, cross his arms, and lie there on the estrada,[4] quite still, until death came. Other times, he had toyed with running the risk of stealing a canoe and fleeing to Manaus.... He had come from his own native land with an uncommon desire for fortune, dreaming of settling down in Sitiá one day with a grassy field and some calves and goats. His reward was to be stuck here in the strange swampy wilderness of an Amazonian backwater, eaten up by 'the plague' and stricken with malaria! But this opportunity that had been offered to him, the opportunity to break even, had revitalised him. He would return to his homeland, God willing!

It had been a long time since he first left the Lower Amazon, where he had spent the initial phase of his exodus as a condemned man. He had worked there for three years without any profit. Apart from a little tapurú, the rubber was weak; it was itaúba. At Lago do Càstanho, he had married that cabocla, a marriageable enticement. She was a temptress who had come to hinder his life: if he had come up here alone to work in the rubber plantations, he would surely be

_____

4. A beaten path through the colocação, the parcel of land assigned to the tapper in the rubber plantation.

back in his beloved Ceará by now. It was true that in Maibi's company life had been sweeter.... However, it had been a mistake. He had managed to extricate himself from this situation, but, having succeeded, he found that he now longed for his beloved cabocla. Ah! her eyes, brown as pajurá[5] juice; her youthful, easy walk like that of a wading bird; ah! her hair, black like the raised feathers cresting the mutum-de-fava;[6] her shapely figure.... The girl's ardent caresses would now be lavished upon another...she would burst into oaths and sighs in the arms of another.... It had been very hard for him to walk away, but 'it was the only way'. So the rubber tapper tried his best to stifle such troubling thoughts....

What is certain is that, when Sabino left the warehouse, he felt weighed down by a heavy burden.

That day, a Sunday in March, was busy in the barracão; the customers from the rubber plantation came to visit and do business. There was a shortage of 'd'água' flour,[7] pirarucu fish and beef jerky, but the 'house steamer'[8] was about to arrive with the supplies. People flocked in, keen and curious about the brabos[9] that the steamer would bring. But deep down they were brought together by the irrevocable need for social interaction, which became increasingly intense in the regime of isolation that ate away at them.

At dusk, a large number of customers filed into the biggest room in the barracão for the dance. The harmonica began to sound out the solemn flat notes of a waltz. The men—in the midst of whom there were only two women—clung to one another in pairs, flailing about dancing on the sagging, warped paxiúba floorboards.[10]

---

5. A fruiting tree found in the Amazon (*Couepia bracteosa*).

6. I.e. the wattled curassow. A bird with impressive black plumage.

7. Coarse flour of inferior quality.

8. I.e. the supply ship belonging to the rubber plantation owners.

9. A regional term for new arrivals to the rubber plantations.

10. The paxiúba is a type of palm tree commonly used to build houses, bridges etc. on plantations.

The gas lamp attached to the rafters was almost lost in the enveloping tobacco smoke. Once the music ceased, there was a loud rumble of conversation and laughter, until the tireless and rasping harmonica groaned on with some new bars.

Late at night, on the Lieutenant's pronouncement—'That's enough for today, guys!'—the room emptied out. The rubber tappers went back to their lodgings. The barracão had become dull and grim, an even blacker shape against the dark night in which the tiny blue diamond of a single neglected star flickered and shimmered.

The first face Marciano saw the next morning was Sabino's. The boss accosted him immediately. 'Are you feeling sorry for yourself? If you want, you can go to another rubber plantation: I don't mind. If you want to stay, you can do that too...I certainly won't forbid it.... Do whatever you like.'

Sabino declared that he had no regrets, that he would not be backing out, and that he wanted to work, but at a spot in the centre.[11] He intended to stay at Paulino's place; Paulino was dying, having been bitten by a tucanoboia snake four days before. The estrada, which would likely yield two and a half jars of rubber sap, was not much, but it all helps. Besides, he was counting on the Lieutenant to give him a hand with a few necessaries. Not much: a fishing net, a pair of blue trousers, 'carapanã'[12] and 'taurina'[13] pills, boxes of bullets, flour, and pirarucu meat; things that a man debased by a such a world could not do without. Should he start clearing the estrada then? In the week ahead he wanted to start 'bleeding the trees'....

The Lieutenant nodded with disproportionate benevolence. 'Oh yes! That's right.... Everything will be arranged.... The "Rio Iaco" will be here in a few days....'

In fact it was a week later that the steamer docked at Soledade, to the excitement of those who had been eagerly awaiting its arrival.

---

11. The 'centre' in rubber plantation terminology means further into the forest, further away from the central node of the barracão.

12. Anti-malaria pills made from a quinine preparation.

13. Pills to combat liver disease.

It took many hours to unload the cargo. Some cattle were thrown from the hatchway into the water where they crashed and promptly swam ashore. Boxes, baskets, bundles, and jugs passed over the gangplank, quickly run over as if they were being shifted by panicked smugglers. In a hectic frenzy, everything was piled up on land in order to be transported to the warehouse, with the exception of the scattered cattle, who nipped at shoots, trimming the reeds at the water's edge.

The personnel that the bookkeeper had gone to Ceará to pick up disembarked along with the cargo. About twenty heads, people from Crato and Crateús. In total, fifty people had been recruited at the port of Camocim. But some had fled in Pará, others in Manaus, and five had kicked the bucket due to fevers.

'Oh! Wicked scoundrel!' was the phrase that the attendant would use at every opportunity while describing to Marciano those involved in the mission with which he had been entrusted. He had complained about it to a subprefect in Manaus, but no one had been sent to track down the men on the run in Mocó.... The whole campaign was in the red to the tune of thirty contos. The bookkeeper also blamed the disaster of the expedition on the casa aviadora,[14] because it had delayed the departure of the ship in Belém, and the manager had 'broken up the group', refusing to advance the borós[15] to cover the needs of the personnel....

In the middle of the night, the moment came when the 'Rio Iaco', steam thunderously spewing from its discharge pipe, its plank retracted and cables untied, gently moved away from the bank. A resounding steam 'siren' whistle echoed ominously, ululating in the wilderness.

After the shout of farewell to the birdcage steamer, life in Soledade resumed its usual course. From the central unit, the barracão, the other units radiated out, the barracas. This sparse and basic

---

14. A credit institution. This credit regime was called 'aviamento', and was made up of networks distributing credit relations. The *casa aviador* would extend credit to a smaller *aviador* and so on until this system reached the primary producers.

15. A form of paper money issued by the municipalities of the sertão.

network formed an organic system, managing to cover large square leagues with the labour of just a few men. Along varadouros[16] and igarapés, goods were transported away by the barracão's workers in jamaxins[17] and canoes.

Before the new workers dispersed, Marciano gathered them all in the vast hall at Soledade and spoke to them. He wanted to see hard work and customers paying off their balances. He was not in the business of lending money. He did not want to hear stories and excuses, he wanted rubber! Disregarding any moral scruples or any care for the conservation of the wealth of the forest that Nature had gifted him, he brutally summed up the absurd program of his exploitation in the following homily: 'Let he who is an armadillo dig; let he who is a monkey climb.' He went on to explain this bizarre motto: he had no qualms about the rubber trees being stripped from root to branch, in a formal decree of extinction. They would build 'mutás': crude scaffolds to allow the jars to capture the precious sap higher up. Or they would use the 'arrocho': a hideous form of constriction, increased day by day so that the trunk, strangled by the garotte, would gather the most valuable sap into its excretions. The boss demanded the maximum product, even at the cost of annihilating the trees, with a formidable brand of ignorance which, if widespread, would result in the liquidation of the principal form of wealth in the Amazon basin, cutting it off at its source.

At the end of these imperious exhortations to crime and recklessness, the brabos went on to hastily settle on the estradas recently opened up by the explorers last winter.

The hustle and bustle of 'getting everyone settled in' finally over, the manufacturing process began. It would continue until the end of the harvest, month in, month out. The Lieutenant, on the Soledade bridge, or sitting on the veranda, reassured of his fortune by a

---

16. Paths along which canoes can be dragged to avoid difficult stretches of river.

17. A basket with handles, made of timbó, in which rubber tappers carry their goods from one place to another.

fat balance with Prusse,[18] yet still calculating the ledger of probable profits and losses, smoked his expensive cigars, scanned the newspapers, or wandered along the riverbanks between uniform hedges of insipid oiranas.[19]

Soledade's barracão overlooked a military observation post on the surrounding floodplain. As if some gigantic plough had driven into the plain, the water worked its way back into the fertilising channel. Tillage in August for Pan's fields…. The forest was painted Veronese green; the sky was watered-down Prussian blue; the hours dripped like thick oil draining through a bleeder; the sun crept through its imperial palaces every day, with the servility of a slave….

It was one empty afternoon, bright and slow, that Marciano spotted a certain canoe rounding the bend of the backwater, heading for the barracão. From the opposite bank it crossed, making ripples in the smooth, grey robe of the river. At the bow, the oarsman was paddling frantically. No sooner had he pulled the boat over than he jumped ashore. It was Sergio, and he was pale and visibly disturbed. Approaching the boss, Sergio told him that he had taken advantage of a few rainy days, when he could not make any cuts in the rubber trees, to make a trip to the 'centre', but that when he had returned, he could no longer find Maibi at home. The cabocla had disappeared; she had left only a petticoat in the marupá trunk. He was exhausted from searching…he would go all the way downriver inquiring…he would even reach Umarizal. Overcome with indignation and anguish, Sergio rushed down the steps of the bridge.

The Lieutenant, his instinct well-honed as a former police officer in São João de Uruburetama, immediately thought of Sabino. Perhaps the jealous Cearense had made off with the girl? It occurred to him to send a trusted man to the centre to see if he could locate the suspect and find anything out on the sly.

---

18. One of the major rubber export companies in Brazil, based in Manaus.

19. A small tree that grows on riverbanks and thrives even when submerged by the flood (*Salix Humboldtiana*).

Sitting on a stool in the kitchen, Zé Magro was cutting and trimming his tobacco leaves, humming quietly:

Migo, migo, migo, migo
This bundle of tobacco,
That I smoke from strand to strand
And chew from plug to plug...

—when he heard that they were calling for him. He responded immediately, and the commotion ceased. After receiving orders and instructions from the Lieutenant, he took his rifle and left.

He jumped across the field in a single bound, crossed the crude bridge, and plunged into the forest, disappearing over the plantation fence. A little later, the watchman came across Sabino, who was leaving the estrada. Sabino was wearing a filthy shirt, his trousers trailing over his rubber-soled feet, and his head was covered in mosquito netting. He had a machete tucked into his belt, a small hatchet and a bucket in his hands. A small bag hung on his flank and there was a rifle slung over his back. The outfit reflected the squalor and risk of the trade.

They struck up a conversation.

'Good morning today? A lot of milk, eh?' asked Zé Magro.

Sabino replied, struggling to control the emotion that threatened to overwhelm him: 'Not really....'. And, trying hard to calm down, he continued, 'I tapped an absolute monster on the estrada there... a good one...enough for twelve bowls. It can fill up a whole flask by itself. I managed to miss the devil before. I passed by and didn't see the brute...and yet it was just past the mouth of the first manga[20] of the estrada.'

The other, surprised at Sabino's serenity, muttered a bewildered reply, making a reference to the whims of the 'mother of the rubber tree'[21] who liked to play at hiding the trees. To disguise his spying, he tried to make a display of curiosity. 'I wouldn't mind taking a look at that tree...if it is as you say!'

---

20. A small path breaking off from the main estrada—see following page.

21. In Amazonian folklore, a forest spirit who protects the rubber tree.

'Well, go on', replied Sabino. 'You'll be amazed. Even though you're no brabo, you'll never have seen anything like it. Just head over to the base of an assacuzeiro tree, after a thicket of "cat's claws", and you'll swear....'

'All right, let me take a look.' And Zé Magro went straight toward the forest behind the smoking hut[22] which marked the end of the estrada.

Sabino watched the spy go; as soon as he had disappeared, he took his head in his hands and began to shake all over, overcome with epileptic paroxysms. He paced to and fro, back and forth, pressing his hands to his chest as if to pull out his innards, and tugged at his hair, sobbing and groaning. He seemed to rush toward the estrada to call someone; then, as if in repentance, retreated into the forest clearing, only to get bogged down in the marsh.... He gave the impression that he was being threatened with a fiery whip by some sinister pursuer. Occasionally this pursuer would catch up with him, making him jump and flail around as he fled from the stinging lashes.

Meanwhile, Zé Magro continued his cautious and suspicious hunt for this supposedly spectacular rubber tree. The leafy estrada is really just a track made while in search of trees to be tapped. However, it almost always forms a polygonal line that eventually closes in on itself. Sometimes smaller polygons break off from it, so-called 'loops', or else simple lines, 'mangas'; but its general outline is always that of a track winding its way around hundreds of trees to be exploited. During the harvest, the seringueiro rushes around it, often before dawn, by the light of his gaslamp, filling the bowls with milk beneath the small diagonal cut, making the appropriate 'arreação'.[23] He will soon return along the same tracks in order to collect the milk from the bowls in his bucket. Early in the morning the rubber-tapper heads back in, exhausted; he still has to smoke the latex in the acrid fumes of the coconuts which burn under the boião pot, punishing his eyes.

---

22. In these 'defumadores', the rubber tappers would smoke the hevea milk, causing it to coagulate. This turns the white sap into the black substance to be transported.

23. Term for the series of blows used to bleed the rubber tree.

In his usual manner, Zé Magro was moving at a rapid pace, barely noticing the assacuzeiro in the tangle of vines, and fell in terror at the unexpected and bizarre spectacle that awaited him. A woman, completely naked, was tied to a rubber tree. In the lustrous frame of her thick black hair, her face was not visible.

Zé Magro came closer, trembling, in order to examine the terrible scene. Astonished, he recognised that the crucified woman was Sabino and Sergio's wife.

Tied to a tree on the estrada with pieces of ambécima, the cabocla's reddened body eerily adorned this plant, which served as a type of pillory. She was like an extravagant orchid, fleshy and dark, growing at the foot of the fateful tree. Over the turgid breasts, over the arched belly, over the stiff legs, a dozen rubber bowls, modelled in dull clay, had been embedded deeply into the flesh. The woman's blood must have filled them and overflowed from them, watering the roots of the living prop that supported the dead woman. The milk in the bowls had curdled—red sernambi....[24]

This spectacle of unprecedented flagellation had the emotive and harmonic grandeur of an immense pagan symbol, resembling a cruel sacrifice offered to some unknown, terrible Babylonian deity— with the slaughtered woman on the tree representing the earth....

And yet Maibi's martyrdom, with her life draining away into the rubber tappers' bowls, was still far less than that of the Amazon, offering itself up as fodder for an industry that is draining it dry. Although motivated by different intentions, in his revenge the seringueiro had sculpted this imposing and flagrant image of its sacrificial exploitation. There was a aura of oblation about this corpse which could be said to represent, in miniature, a greater crime, one not committed out of Love by a single deranged heart, but by the collective Ambition of a thousand souls driven by a universal greed.

Making haste, Zé Magro returned, and when he appeared at the mouth of the estrada he would have been unrecognisable to anyone who saw him. The shock had given a patina to the matt bronze of his

---

24. Naturally coagulated rubber residue.

face. He looked around. He grabbed his rifle, held it close, and fired several times in succession as a signal for help. The dormant forest, in the midday heat, emitted not the slightest murmur. It was immobile, as though turned to marble or hypnotised. Zé Magro cast around yet more. He was so anxious he could not contain himself, and roared, 'Sabino! Hey! Sabino!' Only the harsh cry of a cauré answered the call.

'Sabino!...Sabino!...' he cried again, with greater intensity.

But this time not even the evil hawk responded.

10. Fool's Gold

You are going, you are going too, hapless victim;
The breath of ambition has closed your eyes
        Machado de Assis, 'La Marchesa de Miramar', *Falenas*

While the skipper of the barge, threading the tiller through his hands, sent it to port and starboard to avoid the twists and turns of the current, Vicente Mucuin, leaning on the batelão's bow, gazing sceptically at the unwinding coastline that spread out like a rosary of poetic spots surrounded by greenish patches of muri, Inga trees, embaúbas and taxis....[1]

Since he could not find Gertrudes in Manacapuru, he would follow the beaten track to Maués—the fiefdom of Colonel Tito. It was his land, that dead little town, by the river, slack and vegetating like a frail araçaí tree in the middle of the igapó. In a sad corner, nestled in a quagmire, this place lost in the far reaches of the nation was the supplier of a life-saving food which was produced and manufactured here alone: guaraná.[2] The plant, a thin and sarmentose[3] vine with a delightful scientific name,[4] bears fruit in saffron-coloured clusters, similar to those of the jurubeba that thrives in abandoned fields.

---

1. The ant tree, known for its striking pink flowers (*Triplaris americana*).

2. A climbing plant in the family *Sapindaceae* with orange-red fruit, which contains large amounts of caffeine. The fruit is of major importance in Tupi-Guaraní folklore. (*Paullinia cupana*.)

3. Having stems in the form of flexuous runners or stolons. When the red outer layer of the fruit opens up, the white and black within resemble a cartoonish eyeball.

4. If not *Paullinia cupana*, this may refer to another of its names, *Paullinia sorbilis* (sorbilis means 'suck-upable').

There is a whole hermetic art to the preparation of the chocolate paste to which the little fruits of the sapindacea are reduced, roasted, crushed, and combined with just the right amount of water by a knowledgeable cabocla. It is then shaped into various naive sculptural forms: alligators, inkwells, turtles, walking sticks, fishes, and bunches of grapes. These serve as souvenirs, like those pieces of solidified lava by which we remember trips to Naples, or an object made from olive root that serves as a memento of a stay in Nice or Cannes. The paste, which is very useful, is sold in rolls at a price even higher than 'fina'[5] rubber.

Merchants from Cuiabá travelled in caravans through the hinterland on the most amazing odysseys in search of this nutritious and stimulating paste. They searched for this tonic in the dark zones of river valleys, mysterious, remote, infested with man-eating insects and beasts, sprayed by foam from waterfalls, sheltering in caves, facing more than a thousand dangers over a period of many months, travelling hundreds of leagues all the way to this little Amazonas village. Later on, Lloyd[6] shortened the length of the enormous journey, reducing the number of passages through mountain ranges, gorges and plateaus, which only Friar José dos Inocentes[7] himself, in desperate need of escape, would not have thought absurd.

Why is it that the Cuiabanoa, of all the Brazilian peoples, were the only ones to fall in love with this substance? And how was it that the habit of taking this drink diffused so far from the place that produces it? And that it became so indispensable that men would, without fear, venture out on a journey to rival Livingstone—as if Maués sat

---

5. The term for the coagulated latex of *Hevea brasiliensis*. It is rubber of the highest quality. Rubber that is smoked all the way through without the milk being saturated is called 'fina'.

6. This probably refers to Lloyd Brasileiro, a shipping company founded in 1894, which became a major commercial force across South America.

7. In June 1832, an uprising of citizens and troops declared the Rio Negro region to be an independent province, cutting it off from Pará. Although the rebellion was quashed, Friar José dos Santos Inocentes was sent out to Rio de Janeiro as a representative.

on a stupendous repository of priceless metal, or, even more so, kept within its walls the indispensable element of the life that the people of Mato Grosso lived! No doubt someone, some keen investigator of gaps in the historical record, some maniacal analyst, some grinder of ethnographic minutiae, will come along to explain what obnoxious event originally set off this bumpkin pilgrimage to the backlands Mecca of guaraná....

The caboclo Vicente had the wanderlust of the Cearense. After spending two years cutting rubber in Jatapu, he went on to extract piassava in the upper Rio Negro, on the outskirts of Venezuela. From here he returned to that secretive nest where Colonel Tito dominates with his beady eyes and the commanding profile of a royal hawk.

There was nothing tougher than stripping the Leopoldinia palm of its textile fibres, which coat it all over, from the petioles to the base of the trunk. The bristle, which might have been worn by an evil and repulsive idol, some Kanaka or manitou,[8] is rough and is frequented by spiders, caterpillars, snakes, scorpions, and centipedes. From sun up to sun down, mired in the igapós, the job is an unprecedented punishment for parricides. The hands and face are scratched by the untangling of the coarse lint, which must be torn from the abominable plant. And always the terror of some creature crawling out of the wood, with its teeth out or its poisonous sting at the ready....

Nothing worthwhile had come of it. The caboclo had never seen so much as ten real out of this work, which was like some cruel and refined Chinese punishment. Yet he considered himself lucky. One day, while 'hunting' the pissavas, he came across some shiny stones,

---

8. A pervasive supernatural force among Algonquian groups in Native American theology. 'Manitou might inhabit plants, animals, or inanimate objects, and could be manifest in phenomena such as thunder or earthquakes. Some peoples recognized manitous associated with directions, social groups, or animals, and sought their help with the intervention of religious specialists, who were called powwaws or shamans among the southern New England Algonquians.' K.J. Bragdon, *The Columbia Guide to American Indians of the Northeast* (New York: Columbia University Press, 2001), 18.

clustered in small groups of dark crystals. Surely this was gold, or some other mineral of great value—a real treasure trove!

Feverish, Vicente filled his flask with the glittering mineral. His initial impulse had been to fill a jug, maybe some boxes...but that would be conspicuous. It would be better to hide the find and not reveal the cargo, which would draw the attention of strangers.

He immediately thought of abandoning the harvest and travelling to Maués to tell his wife everything. From there, he would return to Manaus, to find someone he could trust with the secret and sell the stones.

Vicente set off travelling, overloaded with dreams. His imagination worked non-stop. He drew up projects like a madman. The barge, its old engine purring, seemed to be hardly moving. A carará passed by in the azure air: he considered it a pity that he did not have the wings of this bird that could travel so quickly....

Although Vicente kept himself to himself, the crew and passengers were wary of the caboclo. His suspicion of others caused him to withdraw even more deeply. Everyone around him wondered what made him so strange and aloof. Distrust and mystery were written all over his face. The man would not part with a bag that was stuffed full, his only luggage. In it were the stones, Vicente's fortune, the precious flask.

The batelão, tied to the flank of the motor boat by its thick spras, began to creak in the heavy structure of its hull and its arito laurel[9] ribs. The suddenly turbulent waters of the river attempted to separate the conjoined boats. Black spouts sprouted angrily in the shoals and unfathomable whirlpools at the mouth of the Rio Negro. One mighty current was trying to penetrate another in a violent fusion, a battle of two rampaging monsters, tearing each other apart in a swirling of fins and tails in the abyss. The Rio Negro clashed against the claws of the muddied Solimões River, and the fragments were swallowed up by the latter, imposing, resilient, soon resting from the battle, spreading lazily downstream through Lages and Terra Nova.

---

9. (*Aniba puchury-minor.*)

The motorboat, hitched to the batelão, passed through the jolting eddies of waters roughened and enraged by this encounter. Marapatá, a shallow islet prone to taking a bashing, lay on the left, its insignificant undergrowth nourished by the swamp. As clear as in an engraving, the ships at the Manaus harbour could be made out, etched against the backdrop of the bright city. An hour and a half later, at the anchorage, the motorboat was besieged by a swarm of boats, with Portuguese sailors, islanders, amidst invitations and conviviality, making a great racket competing to transport passengers to land: 'Doctor'...'Oh!'...'Sir'...'Doctor!'...'Damn it...!'...'Eh! Boss! don't you want to get ashore?'...'Check out the Estrela-do-Norte!', hotel representatives were announcing: 'The Familiar', 'The Vasco da Gama'....

Two English liners, leaning against the Manaus Harbour pier,[10] were loading and unloading cargo to the sharp and intermittent sound of winches. A steamer from Acre, full of people leaning against the rail and itching to finally disembark, awaited a visit from Health and Customs. Other birdcages either empty or preparing for departure, motorboats, barges, and pontoons lay anchored here and there, reminiscent, with the sight of the Maxim machine guns on a warship sheltered in the same anchorage, of the remainder of a pirate squadron captured and in disarray. Labourers were working on the unfinished pier. The Matriz church rose up, blue, from a belt of almond trees, hibiscus, and eucalyptus. A tugboat came from the mouth of the São Vicente igarapé, towing a pontoon.

Clutching his bag, Vicente joined the other passengers on one of the boats. As soon as he got ashore at the jetty, he tried to find out the date when the steamer on the Maués line would depart. He ran to the agency in front of the Teixeira pier.

The 'Silvério Nery' was departing that same afternoon. Once again, the caboclo stepped onto a deck topped with a small, crooked cage-like structure, his expression as flat as a sole. The steamboat sounded its departure signal and steam and smoke billowed from its

---

10. The Manaus pier was famous because it was built to float on top of barrels in order to rise and fall with the river's tides.

chimneys as it set course for the mouth of the Solimões River after skillful maneouvres in the port. Vicente took a good sip of the cana[11] offered to him by another third-class passenger from Ceará, an old acquaintance, who had some sort of business on the coast of Burrinho. The conversation between them quickly became lively. Memories came flooding back, events tucked away in the recesses of their shared recollections.... The restraint the caboclo had maintained with regard to keeping quiet about his discovery suddenly fell apart in an irresistible confession.

The knowledge of the stones in the waterproof bag ignited a burning interest in the Cearense man. He insisted that Vicente tell him everything. How had he found them? Were there a lot of them? Vicente shared every detail, his happiness overflowing as he recounted his adventure as an accidental novice prospector. No detail was spared. He described how the minerals were arranged in the deposit, the trees surrounding it, and the path to get there through the depths of the forest, after five days of traveling eastward. 'It was very thorny,' Vicente emphasised. The dogs had cornered a pack of little pigs in a patch of caranas. The terrain was ascending; there were no igarapés. The only thing that had saved him from his thirst was the muirátitica,[12] 'a pure spring, trapped in a vine'. The narrative became filled with countless minutiae. He had finally stumbled upon a deep pit, and those scattered stones. So many that you could pick them up by the handful, enough to fill an igarité.

The man from Ceará advised Vicente to return to Manaus as soon as possible in order to find someone who might understand and buy him out. They would then go back to the mine together and bring down as much as they could. He offered to be a partner and would invest some capital. He pleaded...they were friends, after all...Vicente was not to go to Maués, risking the wrath of the old royal hawk.... It would

---

11. Sugar cane liquor or aguardente de cana, the original name for cachaça rum.

12. The caboclo vine. If you cut off the thick twigs of this vine and empty them into a container, you can get fresh, pleasant-tasting water. (*Doliocarpus dentatus*.)

not be wise to delay in this business. The sample could disappear.... Once they both disembarked at Burrinho, they could then take the Autaz service boat back up....

Vicente was convinced.

That night, the little steamboat continued along the Amazon River with the noisy rhythm of its pistons, gears adjusting, the rudder chain creaking across the ropes attached to the tiller.... The passengers slept; a sailor and a pratico[13] were in the bow, and a stoker was in the engine room, keeping watch on his designated four-hour shift.

Filled with curiosity, the Cearense begged Vicente to show him the treasure right there and then. Under the dim, muted light of a ship's lantern, the tiny crystals sparkled in their nervous hands. In the dizzying vertigo of faith and seduction, the gravel had the brilliance of sun shards, dazzling and blinding them.

An abrupt and sudden rocking shook the ship, from the hull's bolts to the tops of the masts that disappeared into the dusky sky. The dishes in a cabinet rattled and glass shattered. A lightning bolt flashed, sweeping the distant banks of the river with sulphurous light. Erratic gusts violently shook the canvas curtains on the decks. The waters swelled and formed deep troughs. The birdcage danced like a fool in the rough waves. The air, electrically charged, was torn apart by the grim clarity of the lightning. Overlapping cracks of muffled thunder rolled. There was no sea more treacherous than this river. In the drowsiness of a calm day it resembled a tranquil pond; no one would think it capable of these hurling waves. The tempestuous Amazon could not be restrained, a frothing madman convulsing in the confinement of his bed. The blades of the propeller, for a moment spinning above the water, conveyed a sudden tremor to the 'Silvério Nery', the kind of tremor that makes the flesh of the shipwrecked quiver at the tragic moment when the ship is lost....

Little by little, the weather calmed down. Its fury, which had been so acute, quickly gave way. An hour of panic among the raging elements,

---

13. A pilot who knows a given steamer route particularly well (someone well-practised on that route).

and the night went back to weaving its moonlit garment with the thread unwinding from the luminous spindle of the crescent moon.

Heralding the day, the rising sun was like a seashell gradually revealing the depths of its pearly hollows.

Having 'called a canoe' by means of incessant whistling, the two men left the birdcage, which had weathered the storm. The stones were placed with sacramental care on the saddle of the montaria. Minutes later, they stood shivering with their cargo at the muddy base of a ravine. Huddled in the house, they exchanged ideas; they settled future arrangements, clarified plans and then came up with new ones until sovereign sleep overtook them.

On the way up to 'Nazareth 2', the man from Ceará would indeed return to Manaus. The very same morning they arrived at his home in Burrinho, the Cearense robbed Vicente, first cutting his carotid artery with a quicé. Resolutely he took the murdered man's body and, in the blink of an eye, hid it in a fold of the flooded forest. He then set off for Manaus with a handful of the stones from the flask.

As soon as he landed, he quickly sought out the home of a doctor whom he knew by name, a knowledgeable and serious young man, much praised by a compadre from Careiro. In no time, he reached Epaminondas Street, in the direction of the 36th barracks. When he found the doctor, he explained the purpose of his visit and began to unravel the intricate knots of a handkerchief. Once the final knot was undone, tiny shiny black cubic crystals rolled out. The doctor looked interested, took a bit of the mineral between his fingers, and examined it calmly.

The man from Ceará, awaiting the examination, trembling, had a pale countenance, marked by emotion.

'Ah!' sighed the well respected man. 'This is pyrites...iron bisulphide.'

And then, glancing at the Cearense, who was bewildered by the scientific terminology, he added, his benevolent smile fading, 'It's nothing. Just rocks. They're worthless. They're everywhere.' And, rummaging through the stones, he explained with scepticism, 'It's possible I'm wrong, but I don't believe there is mineral wealth in this country. They say that in the upper Rio Branco, in the Atuman, in the Madeira....

But all that's really there is a delusion in which spontaneous fantasists and systematic hustlers take pleasure. I know of a Colombian who had some gold flakes from Minas Gerais mixed with pebbles and sand he had brought from Cachoeirinha, and he put the mixture in a jar he had brought back from a trip to the Içá River. I don't know if this "old wives' tale" has caught on. Look, my dear man, the real treasure is this land itself. And it's inexhaustible. A várzea in the Amazon is a true California. Rubber plant, corn, cocoa, beans, sugarcane, cassava, rice...the rest is just Arabian Nights stuff. When it's real gold, there's something fishy going on;[14] be wary of some Colombian's trickery. Well thought-out, persistent work is everything, my friend,' the consultant emphasised. 'Our great vice is to be incorrigible dreamers who put all their faith in chance....'

With a priestly gesture, laying his hands on the shoulders of the confused listener, he continued, 'We have the blood of the poor people who collapsed in the spasm of an enormous illusion—the magnificent and wonderful Orient, and the Africans and Indians, gullible as children.... We must open our eyes and let our hearts expand. Land and sun we do not lack; the rest will be accomplished by the human will that desires to conquer....'

Then there was silence, cut off by the song of the graúna[15] cooing in a small bamboo cage in the parlour.

The doctor passed the valueless pyrites back to the Cearense; the latter, in his disappointment, stammered out some weak, meaningless words.

The caboclo was not there to receive this disheartening news which turned his precious find into dust. The shattered dream would not hurt him. All the diamonds in the world were as nothing to him.

---

14. The Portuguese here is a reference to the phrase 'Aqui tem dente de coelho! [There's a rabbit's tooth here!]'. It refers to having the suspicion that there is a hidden culprit behind something. The expression probably originated in Portugal. It is well known that rabbits wreak havoc in fields and vegetable gardens. So when gardeners found their vegetables destroyed, the most obvious suspect was immediately evoked: 'Damn! Here's a rabbit's tooth!'

15. From Tupi *guira una*, 'black bird'. (*Gnorimopsar chopi*.)

The riches of Golconda[16] were nothing to him, he had all he needed: the gentle and melancholic shade of the cajurana trees that canopied his eternal sleep in the flooded forest. Whether gems or pebbles, it was all the same to him in this world of empty conventions and desires more fleeting than clouds....

16. A reference to the diamonds mined in the Golconda region in India.

11. Verdant Inferno

His heart, burdened by dull amazement, revolts to find itself a
prey to convulsive agony. He seems to experience the pains of
hell while still in this life, and something beyond despair is made
clear to him.

Victor Hugo, *Hans of Iceland*

The birdcage that had left him in the upper Juruá was now just a grey
blur, quickly fading away to nothing, obscured by the lush mass of
canaranas, sororocas, and embaúbas. Souto was now an exile, committed to this struggle, this delirium of exploring the wilderness. The
little boat rushed back downstream. It had been the last to come
up here, in a feat of reckless daring, and was then prompted into a
hurried return by the fear of being trapped by the fast-moving river,
ending up skewered on the trunk of a piranhea tree or run aground
on some beach. If something like that had happened, the boat would
have been in the same position as Souto, stuck waiting for the return
of the flood in order to go back down to Manaus. A fate which could
spell profit and good fortune for an engineer like Souto would have
been costly for the shipowner....

But the hopes that Souto had cherished so dearly deserted his
heart as he watched the boat that had brought him there with the
last of his money disappear on its way back upriver. Its departure
left him with a stunned face awash with bitter tears. Everything was
either gone or left behind, in the mystery of abandonment and longing. He had steeled himself when he had set out into the interior of
Amazonas with all the vigorous ambition of a young man, a recent
graduate. But that image of the steamer leaving had struck a blow

to his armour and, piercing it like an arrow, it broke his heart in two. Beloved memories of his home and his loved ones came to him, forming a sad chorus that bade him farewell, embracing him and utterly demoralising him. At each memory, Souto broke down into irrepressible sobs. Alone! thought the engineer, in indefinable rage and grief. In his frustration and dejection, his overwhelming, childlike weeping brought everything together into a single crisis which shook him to the core, leaving his nerves abuzz. His friends and family may as well have been on another planet, or from another life. If any illness came upon him, the remedy, perhaps, would be to rot in some ravine, as so many others had before him....

It was remarkable that these thoughts had only begun to discourage him now. He had embarked in Manaus in high spirits, only to disembark like this, vulnerable and in pain. In an imaginative diversion appropriate for mending his frayed spirit, he went back over the twenty-six days that had passed from leaving that city to arriving up here. He remembered everything in great detail. He had embarked under the blazing midday sun. The ship was bursting full of cargo, stocked up to its maximum official capacity. Two hundred men were squeezed in together in a space that was not fit for a hundred, in absurd squalor amidst sacks, coffins, oxen, and jugs. The hammocks, arranged in quincunx, were a tangle, overlapping one another, some even draped over the loins of the cattle. A man had died after being impaled by one of their horns in the hammock in which he slept. A whole herd of cattle squeezed onto a ghost ship, only to be thrown into a vortex. Together with the herd, a cargo plundered by corsairs. Thus the birdcage rode along on the Solimões, making slow progress, bumping into floating islands of plant matter, scraping against floating tree trunks, keeping to the shore to avoid the impulses of the majestic and deep current. Dolphins leapt out of the water to starboard. At dawn one day, in a deluge of mist that was like the smoke from an entire forest burning, they paused until the humidity had dissipated before entering the Juruá. This river was a parody of the other, the same monotony, the same black and smoky green, only narrower. Since it was March the flood was at its height, lending the whole landscape a watery appearance. Cattle were herded together in isolated corrals. In Mauichi, the tops of the crosses in the cemetery were underwater. There was often no land available to bury those who died aboard. The river had to be searched for a grave; since it was all one vast grave, there was no place for one dead person. Stopping at Nova Fortaleza, a rubber plantation owner came aboard. Talkative and rather pedantic, he regaled the first mate with stories, interrupting himself frequently with a bombastic laugh so loud that it rumbled out across the deck. Seventeen days were spent in this labour of negotiating between shorelines, shallows, and oxbow lakes, always the same, with an eternal succession of clouds of mosquitos and black flies in the huts and barracões where they got their firewood or dropped off cargo, and at the other stops they made to harvest grass for the cattle or to spear fish. There was a variety to the names written on the signboards of the barracões, but what they designated was always the same sort of thing, whether they were made of brick or of paxiúba. The fantasies of the occupants or owners, or else their memories or their sentimentality, came into play, prompting them to inscribe the riverbanks with an abundance of marginalia both touching and bleak: *Altarnira, New Paris, Let It Speak, Mirage, Good Place, Santa Helena.* Yet this long slog along the river, which seemed endless, had not really bored Souto. It was, after all, a novelty. Although the spectacle was broadly the same, it was embellished with a thousand different details: the maguari stork perched on a mulateiro,[1] the boat taking on firewood, some jaburus fishing at the mouth of an igarapé, the racket made by a startled flock of curicas or parrots, the mournful strains of an accordion, capybaras fleeing, seringueiros celebrating, waving from the land to the 'braves' on the deck....

It was this look back across the panorama of the journey that had led to Souto's present hypochondriacal breakdown, from which he finally distracted himself by watching the sunset. The sun was like a smouldering ember that could not even ignite the handful of fluffy

---

1. A canopy tree indigenous to the Amazon rainforest, it is also known as Pau-Mulato (*Calycophyllum spruceanum*).

cloud lint beneath which it was being extinguished.... A blue heron was belatedly seeking shelter for the night in the secrecy of the igapó. Nature had a moment of calm, in the splendour of its warmth, light, and vegetation. This ended up restoring his nerve.

When dinner was announced, with monkey and quatipuru[2] on the menu, he responded to the insistent invitation with renewed spirit.

The engineer spent the next day checking his luggage, taking notes, and making arrangements. Only days later did he finally manage to obtain one canoe and two more rowers (in addition to Miguel, whom he had brought with him). One thing after another.... Bored by the delay, he felt glad when, on the first bright morning in April, he finally felt the canoe moving away toward the Juruá-Mirim, to the rhythm of energetic paddling, and found himself huddled under its straw canopy, which was supposed to protect him from the caustic sunshine.

The igarapé was an offshoot from the river. The trees on the banks seemed gigantic; they gained extra height in perspective, owing to the narrowness of the gorge they flanked. Taking advantage of the black stripes of shade cast across the shimmering stream, the rowers he had acquired at the mouth, who were both from Ceará, were constantly talking, halting the movement of their oars. One of them, Chico Brabo, cultivated his own dialect, inventing terms to fill the gaps in the meagre standard vocabulary he had learnt: food was 'trupizup', arrangements offering little or no gain were 'atibisquite' deals.

It was thus, amidst Miguel's respectful silence and the jabbering of the other men, that Souto arrived at a deserted little shack, smothered between old pacoveiras. The banana plantation pressed in on the hut; the forest suffocated the banana plantation; and, in turn, the sky crushed the forest. This was Souto's first landing, at the remote confluence of the Solimões.

After devouring the canned food—the 'trupizup'—everyone took to their hammocks to sleep. A dense cloud of tiny catuquin mosquitos danced along with the oil flame flickering at the top of the lamp. The philosopher, in a corner, was absorbed in a crude commentary

---

2. The Brazilian squirrel (*Sciurus aestuansam*).

on the inequality of human fortunes. Eventually, his words met with no response. Miguel snored and the other, Simeão, remained deliberately mute. Finally, the premises of a syllogism dwindled into a snore.

The engineer was unable to sleep. His hearing seemed to have become keener owing to the isolation; the wind, which entered freely through the gaps in the hut, was apparently causing a stir in the surrounding forest. There were sounds of crashing, whistling, buzzing, pattering, and screeching.... At times the whole forest seemed as though on fire, crackling, and huge tree trunks would break and fall; at others, avalanches would rumble on, pizzicatos were plucked on cello strings, violas and double basses were bowed. The sounds of axe blows, screeches, piping and cymbals could be heard. The feral hooting of owls could be made out amid this concert. The 'mother-of-the-moon'—the sarcastic urutau[3]—laughed at them dismissively. Accompanying her at various pitches were the jacurutús,[4] the 'rip-shrouds',[5] the bacuráus,[6] the ducucús and the acuráos.... The forest laughed, the forest cried.... The convulsing fingers of a delirious virtuoso touched the infinite strings of that great emerald harp, plucking out harmonious or incoherent chords and syncopations from it, in the confused execution of the most terrifying of symphonies. Schumannian accents, the solemn gravity of Berlioz, dissipated into crazy dissonances, shocking arrhythmia.... At one moment Souto heard, at first indistinctly, like a whisper, a great groaning, as though from many human chests breathing out heavily. Then the hoarse wheezing sounds became more pronounced. All that remained in the tumult was that monstrous groan, which seemed to be coming from all the trees in unison, in the dormancy of the vast night—it was the guttural sound of the howler monkeys, probably at the edge of a neighbouring igapó.

---

3. A nocturnal bird in the genus *Nyctibius* which is the subject of many tales in Brazilian folklore.

4. The great horned owl (*Bubo virginianus*).

5. Amazonas slang for the barn owl.

6. Tupi for nightjar.

The jostling, stentorian pack of simians, bellowing in chorus, ended up lulling the engineer to sleep; he woke up to his morning coffee at the threatening dawn of the new day. Urus warbled melodiously, imitating the trills of the rustic flutes of fauns, performing a scherzo. Thick, cold dew dripped from the tips of the palms onto the eaves.

Within an hour, the montaria had resumed its slow pace. A lumbering steed, and badly built—one of the comrades aptly named it 'Tortoise'. Miguel steered carefully, avoiding the rough parts of the course; but the plodding reptile, with some effort, followed the winding cord or the arc of the inflections, along beaches and ravines. The twists of the river were like a snake, coiled up and frozen before attacking.

Two days later, these bowed lines and curved stretches finally paid off: they reached Boa Vista, crowned with manioc, papaya, and reeds, where they were joined by another canoe and three 'rope men'.[7]

Further on, from the Tamboriaco upwards, Souto had to keep track of the topography. And it would still be sixteen hours of heatwaves and flies before they reached the mouth of the Tamboriaco. It was therefore necessary to press on. When they reached that destination, the safest thing would be to walk quickly. To keep danger at bay, it was prudent to travel at full gallop.

The travellers spent the afternoon and evening in a small hut next to a verdant swamp, where all the blackflies and horseflies had gathered to audition victims. This dwelling-place of calangos, tijubinas, and skittish geckos, built from paxiúba trees with its crumbling, burrowing cauaçu roof, was in this state because of the corrupting influence of the swamp. A few manioc plants and a bunch of poorly grown banana trees, the only agriculture around them, seemed to be suffering from the miasmatic pond, which was only half a dozen metres long, and served as a swimming pool for a group of frogs jumping and floating, croaking in unison to the marshy, easy melody repeated in the obsequies of the twilight hours.

The prospect of sleeping there gave Souto the creeps. The murky little marsh obsessed him; and, to chase away black ideas, he began to

7. 'Homems de corda': manual workers employed to serve on ships.

read Júlio Ribeiro's *A Carne*,[8] which he had found, to his surprise, in the fantastical hut. This grammarian's[9] book, flawed as it was, lived and breathed the energetic and intense atmosphere of São Paulo, so much in contrast to this dank corner where the lethal effluvia of dead water draped everything with a funereal veil. Some evil genius loci who dwelled in the slime must have left this book in the shack, in order to offer its guests the ultimate vision of life in the images of its bizarre romance, the principal symbol of which is the luxuriant body of Lenita.

Chico Brabo, stretched out in his Tucum fibre hammock, chanted a Nagô song. In its languorous rhythms, the barbaric melody from Africa bore the unfathomable sadness of a slave ship, one with a withered sail, adrift in the rotten calm of the sea....

The next morning the work would begin. Right in front of the shack, gloomily decorated with swampweed, the initial stake was pounded in. There was no ceremony. Three sticks from a branch had been picked up nearby and, with special notches carved into them, were sunk into the ground like gigantic teeth, poisonous with impossibly cruel venom which would cause this land deadly seizures as it was sucked dry by future exploitation. The legs of the compass tripod spread out like those of a huge spider; Souto peered into the prism eyepiece, making a brief note in his notebook. He knocked back the pinnules. Then he took the Lugeol[10] scope out of the box and aimed it firmly at the same spot where the red and white crosshairs were located, decorating the chest of the decrepit forest with an extravagant plaque.

At that early hour of the morning, the deep, infected chalice of the mire exuded a thin mist. With only the first stake driven in, the scope put away, and the legs of the compass tucked in, all to be carried off to the next station, the sun was rising over the top of the forest, shining down in rays that dissipated the fog with blazing swordstrokes.

---

8. A work of naturalist fiction from 1888 that proved particularly controversial upon its release owing to its eroticism.

9. Ribeiro was a renowned philologist, notably publishing the *Grammatica Portugueza* (1881).

10. A French brand of theodolite.

The plots to be demarcated followed the twists and turns of the igarapé. The route would bring them to Nova Vida by the end of the afternoon.

Huge logs, entwined with branches, stood in the way. This meant that the crowded igarapé had to be repeatedly cleared with a machete. When travelling from the mouth, this task was necessary. In order to navigate, it was necessary to cut everything down. The water, swirling through the forest and pulling it in at every turn, with the resolute intention of obstructing the natural lines of penetration, made the axe even more indispensable than the oar.

Faced with a behemothic tree trunk blocking their passage, the montarias had to be unloaded and made to pass underneath it in the water. They were then dislodged and refilled with their cargo, which had been temporarily deposited on land. On other occasions, the men covered the back of trunks with embaúba bark so that the boat would slide over with a push, thus passing the abrupt and immovable obstacle.

The branches of spindly taboca bamboo trees hung down, assaulting the passengers, dangling their hooks. Their treacherous aculei could tear clothes, lance the skin, or gouge the eyes.

Everything conspired to make Souto's suffering more acute. The blackflies were pleading to be taken on the journey, and as they irritated the epidermis of his hands, with the nape of his neck protected by a providential mosquito net, the obsessive memory of the lethal lagoon returned....

At night, at Nova Vida, the engineer found his body bruised and his joints aching. He hastily swallowed a quinine capsule. A slight shiver ran through his tired muscles. That sleep the day before, in the shack where he found *A Carne* and the muddy pool! The heat rose to his head with a strange burning sensation...his mouth was dry....

Souto had got up late. As the morning faded, he had felt better and had nervously jumped out of the hammock. Miguel had brought him boiled cassava and a tapir stew; he had barely touched the meal, but had savoured a few sips of steaming coffee.

However, the fight had to continue. Souto would not give up. It was an opportunity for him, and perhaps would pass off without any adverse consequences. He had to overcome whatever was put in his way. Courage was still the best remedy. Fatalities caused by fear itself were very common. Avoiding a morbid attitude, that was the problem. Since Souto had managed to overcome the vague fears in his soul to reach the top of this sertão where he had been handed the chance to seek fortune and then enjoy it among his own people in the south, there was no real reason to be discouraged. He felt much better.... He ordered his comrades to get their montarias ready.

From station to station, the journey continued that day with the same sights along the way: a procession of caustic blackflies and burning sun and the networks of gnarled trees blocking the way.

For the first time, a waterfall presented a rumbling and splashing obstacle. Everyone had to wade into the cold water of the igarapé, leaving the fragile boats, held by ropes, to ride the rapids alone. Luckily they survived the seething froth and foam.

Every now and then, to the right or left, there were the pronounced tracks of tapirs and pigs, or a flowering manacá tree.

Hidden in the dark of the entangled branches that lined the ravines were primitive constructions: tapiris. Souto could clearly distinguish those made by his Peruvian countrymen. These constructions, finished in a framework, had different designs, but the same purpose: that of providing rest for the night. The Peruvian tapiris expressed the precarious nature of their use by nomads. They marked the entry into the rubber zone, in those backwaters of tributaries on the right bank of the Ucaiali. They were the ideal temporary accommodation for a day's work. You cannot conceive of anything simpler: six poles about three feet high, stuck into the ground, supporting an improvised straw canopy.

The cauchero does not build palaces: in his yards he plants plentiful yuca and plantain; this he does to excess. What he wants is to pass through; but keep in mind that in this onwards rush there are forced stopovers. Off we go! The axe and the ubá canoe are the two emblematic instruments of his profession. One destroys, the other transports.

The tapiri is the sign of the union of these two operations, which sum up the devastation wrought by the cauchero. It is the only fixed element, albeit one with the fragile consistency of a spider's web or an armadillo burrow.

Souto, in physical discomfort that he was struggling to subdue, was lost in brooding and reflection.

That day, with its horrible heat and its plague of mosquitos, ended at the mouth of the Funil, the next in a hut that was almost a tapiri: half a dozen paxiúbas, with about as many jaci leaves covering them. The hut was inhabited by a caboclo from Parintins, who was unusually playing the role of someone from Ceara, here in the sombre depths of this rubber-bearing igarapé.

The tapiri dweller was out when Souto and the men arrived, and they immediately went to their quarters. Soon a rifle shot resounded in the forest, with a roaring crash. The guests had barely set up their hammocks and lit a fire with sticks to heat up the 'Paredão' bean stew and the pickled shrimp, when the caboclo appeared, bent over completely under the weight of a formidable peccary. The hunter had left his victim's intestines in the bush to lighten the load. In a frenzy of joy, the comrades greeted the arrival of the carcass with loud cheers: 'What a man!' 'Look at the size of it!'

Like the chimney of a huge lamp, the sky consumed the flames of the sunset to draw off the smoke of night, which fell suddenly.

Souto, prostrate in the hammock, felt a throbbing in his temples. His lips were dry, chapped by the inner fire that burned him all over. While the caboclo and Simeão slaughtered the pig, a certain excitement running through the group in front of this 'fresco', Souto was putting up a tremendous fight against the discouraging thoughts that attempted to invade him in his fever. All night long, however, he saw horrors; sometimes in fire, sometimes in ice, in intense cold, his body seemed to plunge into abysses, or to be flattened by tremendous landslides; the placid igarapé ran deep into the earth, along a spiral, escorted by a double row of monsters that spewed flames....

The whole night was spent in chills, burning sensations, and the terrors of delirium. Miguel approached, from time to time, examining and looking after his boss: 'Calm down, doctor', he advised, with a short caress.

In the morning Souto's eyes were framed with a heavy bistre, his face carved in rough lines, livid and lean.

When the montarias set off to work, the day was high, but between the rock walls, in the complete shade of the canopies supported by the vaulted ribs of branches over the shallow, calm and beautiful stream, it gave the impression of being late. Large blue butterflies passed by slowly, pirouetting, swaying listlessly in the dim light.

Soon, Souto was standing next to the instrument's tripod, resting on the sandy ground of a small beach, closing and putting away his notebook. Black bees, small and sluggish, harassed him. Blackflies covered his hands like a pair of gloves filled with scalding sparks. He could not go on. He had fallen midway through his journey. At last, the returning fever overcame him. And with a shiver passing through all of his tired limbs, with involuntary enthusiasm he ordered an immediate return. He would wait for the affliction to clear at Nazareth, at the mouth of the Funil....

At the mercy of the swift current, with quick and even strokes of the oars, the little canoes travelled back as if keen to save the engineer. When they arrived at Funil, the 'aviado'[11] piously sheltered the sick man in a mediocre shack that languished lugubriously in the shelter of a meagre grove of embaúbas.

There was already a newly arrived rubber tapper, one of the aviado's clients, who had brought the rubber peles[12] he had harvested from the igarapé by water all the way from his shack in the 'centre'[13] to the bank of the Juruá-miri. He came herding this floating flock, which

---

11. A figure in the rubber industry who serves as an intermediary between the boss and the rubber tappers themselves (a certain number of whom the aviado will have on account). See 116n14.

12. Blocks of raw rubber prepared for transport, weighing around 40 kilos.

13. Rubber tapper slang for the interior of the rubber plantation where individual tappers are stationed. The rubber plantations comprised a 'centre' and a 'margin'.

the water carried along, sometimes losing the strange animals into coves. He would then have to seek the dark balls, which liked to linger behind trunks, or hide in matupá.[14] With a piece of wood he guided them along the meanders of the route which they were taking, urging the stragglers back onto the blind path of the flock, trawling them along in the current.

He had finally managed to gather them all together, except for two smaller ones.

This odd shepherd boy returned to his hut in the centre of the plantation, carrying the jamaxim on his back weighed down with goods that the 'aviado' had supplied him with; Souto remained, waiting for his health to improve. Some days were bad, others not so bad. On those days, Souto took the opportunity to map out the work done, or to observe the sun at the appropriate heights so as to determine the local magnetic declination. He still had faith, he still believed.... It would pass. Quinine would triumph...but Souto was becoming ever leaner. Each new day of attacks caused a decline in energy and a loss of muscle. Souto spent eight days like that in Funil, in delirium, with no appetite, and experiencing only fleeting periods of calm. And all the while he wasted away.... The 'aviado' recommended a return to Juruá.

'Outside the doctor will get better...there are more resources....'

In the end the engineer decided to go back down. He recognised the need for this sacrifice: the door to happiness, to have felt it open, and then, when he was outside, to see it close on its hinges.... However, perhaps he would get back on his feet and try again to fulfil his professional obligations to his clients. The poor fellow was vainly jiggling the handle of that door....

With each hut he passed on his way back to Juruá, the illusion of recovery suffered a blow. That hut had long since been abandoned to the thickets, alongside the putrid ooze of the swamp. Souto recognised the nefarious place with his own eyes, which burned as he rounded a bend in the igarapé with crumbling edges. As it suddenly

---

14. A matupá is a floating island of vegetation growing on blocks of soil on the Amazon river system. They can be up to three metres across.

disappeared astern, he thought he was rid of the phantasm once and for all. But it only really left him when one day, in the midst of Chico Brabo's loud monologue—'...rivers are the veins of the earth...'—the Juruá appeared before the two slender prows of the montarias.

The confluence of the Juruá-miri and the Juruá is like a son embracing his father. They merge affectionately in this expansive embrace, a long arm clasping the beloved to its breast. The igarapé must share the feeling of those who reach the river through it: the consoling joy of arrival, after the sombre enjoyment of a dreary life confined to the oppression of a forest.

The prodigal returns, strewing around sandbanks as he goes...languishing in the anxiety that overwhelms him, flitting between bouts of fatigue and dizzy rushes of madness, hungry and passionate by turns, in a reprieve from the calamity that afflicts him, spluttering and weakened, enthralled by a dream that absorbs him entirely....

It was not until the end of July that the steamers would begin to advance up the Riozinho da Liberdade in order to help with the harvest. From the last fortnight of March until that date, the water runs out through the rip in the river; and the punishment for any late boats is to be stuck at the top of the beaches in the dry, their hulls propped up. All around, the maize sprouts, the beans blossom, and the pumpkins and watermelons spread out, ripening their huge fruits on the sand, planted by the boatmen, newly sedentary ad hoc farmers.

Consequently, there was no hope for Souto, whose condition was worsening, of being picked up by one of the liberating, providential birdcage boats. He had therefore decided, leaving the rest of the gang in the lurch, to continue down the Juruá to find a better route, with only Miguel to lead the horse.

The tenacious, rapid, raging fever was relentless. The episodes did not choose a particular time; they assaulted Souto constantly, with the unbridled vigour of an insatiable rage. In the rare instances when the ailment subsided, the engineer would rise from the canoe and, leaning on the awning, would gaze out at the grimy riverbank, which had been shaped into a uniform, infinite furrow....

Nor did it even look like the same route he had travelled up in the birdcage. The ravines had risen up dramatically: the sands on the beaches favourable to being towed had grown, contained in a larger frame. In front of each shack was parked, sometimes stranded, the little house of a floating toilet. Along the banks, the paxiúbas, Martius' iriarteas, lined up in columns, with their spreading capitals of spathes and bronzed palms.

In that monotonous succession, an endless stretch of white beaches and dark straits, minimal incidents distracted Souto: a wrecked boat without an awning, all decked out, with the remains of railings sticking out at the crumbling edges; a sloth in the embauba trees; a tracajá turtle diving; seagulls flying about, shrieking shrilly; a boa constrictor asleep in the sun; a slow-moving flock of cigana birds intruding into the low branches of the bushes; a savvy band of cuxiú monkeys, shrieking, fleeing through the high branches....

On every beach where crops were growing, a scarecrow was set up. It was necessary to frighten off tapirs and capybaras, as well as macaws, 'papa-arroz' seedeaters, widowbirds, and striped cuckoos.... Rubber tappers delighted in inventing these absurd structures, which had the practical aim of driving off the quadrupeds and birds, all of which were harmful to plants and grain.

The simulacra ranged from a simple stick on which a cloth, flag or sheet was hung, to an arrangement which looked like a man wearing a tall hat.

Because of the easy farming, here where the water was responsible for tilling the soil and the seringueiro for sowing, it could be said that these were the only people in the region: immobile, punctilious, extravagant, paralysed, mute, assuming the spasmodic postures of a Saint Vitus dance between the maize and the stalks of the bean plants.

In the end, the stoic gallery of grotesque figures in the river's laps was of great interest. One, bent crookedly, was hooked to a cross, a sacrilegious mockery of holy martyrdom; another, wrapped in a cloak, seemed to be gloomily inspecting the crops; another looked like a soldier on guard duty; yet another was masquerading as a woman, cradling a child....

A great deal of imagination had gone into fashioning these shabby homunculi and animals, beings made of sticks and rags. When the wind came, many of the crude dolls came to life. They would swing like hanged men, the rags of their sleeves, skirts, or cloaks flapping distressingly; they would waddle about, strutting in a macabre burlesque. Simple flaps at the end of their arms gave the illusion of handkerchiefs being waved at an anguished farewell, or of banners torn in some strange gale; those that imitated wings fluttered, and those that mimicked arms waved. In the grey of the evening these garish mannequins would turn black, resembling Goya's charcoal drawings....

For a whole week the 'Tortoise' passed by that extravagant patrol of crop guardians on the riverbanks.

In the sparsely cleared plain, at the mouth of the Moa, a camp was being set up for army personnel who, like jabotis tortoises, or guaiamun crabs in a mangrove, were off to carry out operations on the Amônia. Notes of bugle call broke into the sound of Argentine accents in the wooded area: Souto was amazed at this unexpected sight of platoons and military discipline. The garish red of the uniforms and the white of the tents pampered the forest with their unfamiliar sheen.

A fellow student, an ensign, recognised the engineer. He invited him to jump ashore; he showered him with the attentions of a nurse and a brother.

Souto, however, disliked this narrow circle of labour: the clash of human passions in the virginal expanse of a wilderness. While the soldiers had a good deal of devotion and good humour, the officers were melancholy, complaining about everything, cursing each other, plotting intrigues, or discussing politics. A laxity of soul characterised these individuals, who, for the most part, evidently lacked a complete and rigorous physical and moral training. They were soldiers, and yet what the profession had in store for them in terms of suffering and discomfort made them bitter, twisting them up with resentment!

Commanding the guard, ensuring the continuity of the patrol, or attending the daily orders, in this they create the ability to define their duties, to guide their ideals and to make their lives their own! The country should not worry about translating weapons, uniforms,

vehicles, and manoeuvres from German and French; it should prepare its soldiers for Defence and Death, in the worship and training of
serene dedications that demand nothing for their sacrifice.... Irritated
by these thoughts, the engineer left the expeditioners' barracks as
the morning sky reddened to the shrill dawn reveille. Its rhythm was
excruciating. It seemed to express the deep sorrow of those men in
uniform who, cast out from their homeland, had been discharged into
the Amazonian mire. The forest and the river drank in the poignant
melody of the bugles.

Flowing down a drainage ditch, the waters continued to clear the
way for Souto's montaria, until, at his command, Miguel pulled it over
to a steep ravine littered with membeca grass and shameplant, its
crumbling slope scarcely visible.

Leaning on Miguel, Souto was just able to climb the bank, overwhelmed by a terrible feeling of weakness. He dragged himself up
the steep slope like a bleeding steer, thrust into the butcher's maw.
In the ravine, a capitari tree was tinged with golden yellow flowers. In
the courtyard, the juritis that had been chirping scrambled toward the
safety of the arbuscles, startled. With great difficulty they reached
the platform of the jarina hut, which, amidst the forest, was covered
with the beautiful blossoms of a large rosebush.

That ruin, appalling in its misery and abandonment, was decked
out with corollas, all of which were red, their mouths assuming a
divine smile, laughing at their petals flattened against the sad soul
of the abandoned house. And the roses continued to laugh, until
they burst into mockery of the ill fortune that had just arrived, as if it
had specifically come to seek them out, to seek succour in them and
perfume itself with them!

Whose romantic and loving hands could have planted them, with
the extreme, delicate fantasy of lasciviously populating the solitude
of a rubber 'smoker' with a carnival of flowers in a fairy garden? Rough
and battered hands, rubber tappers' hands, had no doubt weeded the
soil in which the seedlings of these roses had been planted around
the hut, day in and day out. Only for the despised shack to have fallen
to pieces, helpless, piece by piece, under the December showers and

the whipping winds.... In despair, the neglected rose bushes had grown furiously, in the cool of the rain, in the warm lull of the trade winds, receiving the kisses of the solitary and voluptuous dusk, embracing one another as the wind blew, in an affectionate and carnal intertwining of calyxes and branches.

This straw-covered ranch, a grave decorated in spring.... Perhaps the eerie hands of witches would gather the flowers, in the middle of some night of wonders, for sabbath garlands; perhaps Dantesque shadows of lovers, imprisoned in the shack, would adorn themselves with the roses, consoling themselves in the sumptuous blossoming forth of their banishment....

Miguel set up his sick master's hammock and went to prepare the fire.

Two chirping nightingales hopped about along the joint on the straw roof of the hut. Black, bloodthirsty horseflies buzzed around. Exhausted by the tremendous fever, Souto could not wake up. He lay heavily in the hammock. He seemed alive, but only because of his painful, gasping shortness of breath. His drowning body was burning on an invisible pyre.

Outside, in a similar blaze, nature too was burning feverishly. The sun poured a translucent, molten metal over the hut and its rose garden. The glory of the day expressed itself through this desperation to set everything ablaze. That corner of the earth was aglow with fire.

The mirror-like water of the river was liquid steel, bubbling out of a furnace, pouring into the mould. No leaf stirred—all were insensate in the general inertia. In delightful swirls, the slow smoke from the fire, which Miguel had stoked, drifted with some difficulty into the furnace-like air. Cicadas hissed, hidden in the backdrop of the forest, chirping the musical motif of their bucolic song in prestissimos and ralentandos....

As the blazing sun went down, the day's flamboyant pomp faded, darkening; its shining golds became dull and its diamonds were radiant.

Seeing that his boss was quieting down, Miguel hurriedly swallowed his snack and went out to explore the neighbourhood, looking for someone to go with him to assist the sick man. There would probably be someone to help....

In Miguel's absence, the wretched Souto suddenly got up from the hammock. He was on fire. Having climbed down from the platform into the middle of the rose garden, he flailed around, in convulsive movements, in a delirium of activity, pointing menacingly at the trees around him. He was choking on repeated phrases, raving in whispers: 'My land...my...my land, where I came from....' At a certain moment he threw himself at the roses and ripped them from their stems, cutting himself on the thorns. He tried to cover himself with the torn flowers; he held them to his head, attempting to crown himself with them in undeserved anacreontic triumph. He immediately threw them down, then gathered them up, kissed them and tried to crush them with his feet. Lamentably wounded. Souto stumbled and struggled through the rose garden, deflowering it, cutting it down in a whirlwind.

Just as Miguel arrived, accompanied by a rubber tapper, he fell back into the rose bed, belonging now to the forest, wedded to the river:

'Verdant...verdant...inferno!'

The two recent arrivals ran over in pity. His bloodied hands and face gave the impression that this fight with an invisible, despicable adversary had been fought tooth and claw. As he was being lifted, breaking into a smile of relief at the frenzied tensing of his muscles, the engineer died, there, amidst the roses.

There was no echo to pick up and return the bitter words from the lips of the Vanquished. The surrounding land had been labelled and branded: VERDANT INFERNO!

Yet this land, which in killing the adventurer had also lavished him with roses, might have responded: 'I forgive you and I understand the stigma you place upon me. I was a paradise. There is no better, more abundant, more blessed homeland for the native race. Through me these tribes wandered, in the sublime expression of their instincts of conservation, free in the floodlands throughout the river basins. Even today, the caboclos, a virile and helpless remnant among the wreckage of the invasion, live in silent resignation, adoring me, saying a last goodbye to their Edenic resting place, their blessed landscape, their peaceful retreat, in the fatalistic and venerative tradition of the indigenous peoples from which they came. Faced with the failures of the greedy White man, the native will murmur: "We are suffering here, but we can still hold on...." If not a paradise, I will be a purgatory for them, one in which they will atone for their powerlessness while Justice is mercilessly delayed. They will be rehabilitated, in a nutshell, by recalling their story of obscure heroism in the struggle against the social misfortunes that will crush them completely. The Amazon is a green Hell...a verdant inferno for the modern explorer, that restless vandal, the beloved image of the lands from which he came fondly guarded in his soul, yearning with passion to dominate the virgin land that he barbarically violates. I resist the violence of these rapists.... But, finally, although this verdant inferno is a Gehenna of tortures, it is also a place of hope: I am the land promised to superior people, strengthened, vigorous, endowed with determination, intelligence and money; and who, one day, will come to establish the definitive work of civilisation in my bosom, a work which at this moment the first immigrants, humble and poor pioneers of the present, are confusedly sketching out amid blasphemies and gnashing teeth. A poor Jesuit predicted to me, in the cold darkness of a jail cell, that I would be "the delight of men, the delight of life and the envy of the world".[15] Others will come, the lucky ones, once the land has been sown and cleared, to lay the deep foundations of the city where the temporary dwellings of the 'settler' once were. Such tears and suffering are the hallmarks of that transitory period before victory.... I cannot be defeated blithely, just like that.... I demand the same sacrifices as the ancient gods: blood and death. Atonement, however, is worth apotheosis. Let a Poet commemorate, in the splendour of some perfect stanzas, the Victims and the Defeat; the closing of the poem will allude to my Destiny, to the glory of the MOST FERTILE VALLEY—Kingdom

---

15. A reference to Padre João Daniel, author of *Tesouro descoberto no máximo rio Amazonas* (*Treasure Discovered in the Upper Reaches of the Amazon River*) (1757–1776).

of Flowing Waters, Garden of Orchids and Palm Trees, Empire of the Rubber Tree and the great Uaupé!....'

The uncompromising land, reassured and disdainful in its noble prophetic serenity, would go on: 'Oh! Unfortunate invader! You are uprooted, discontent, cursing, but you are fertile.... I am defiled by you, but what does it matter? Impassive though I am, I await the generations that will follow, singing, the chariot of my triumph!'

Yet the innocent earth was silent, in that silence of uncreated worlds; and man lay motionless in a tranquil sleep, in the peace of a Nature indifferent to Ignominy and Scorn....

As the afternoon drew on, the caboclo Miguel began to slowly dig a grave a few fathoms from the shack.

On the Authors, and the Language of *Verdant Inferno*

Alberto Rangel (1871–1945), a military engineer, undertook several surveying expeditions into the rainforest as Secretary of Lands, Mines, Navigation, and Colonisation for the Amazonas State Government. The combination of these experiences with his interest in literary experimentation led him to record them in the highly original collections *Inferno verde* (1908) and *Sombras n'água* (1913), which bring ethnographic and scientific rigour together with an impressionistic prose style. Some of his earlier stories were published in the Curitiba review *O Cenáculo*,[1] associated with the Paraná Symbolist Movement.[2] Because of his adoption of anti-republican ideas, Rangel lived in self-imposed exile in Europe from 1907 until returning to Brazil in 1942.

Euclides da Cunha (1866–1909) is one of Brazil's most famous authors, widely celebrated for his *Os Sertões* (*Rebellion in the Backlands*), published in 1902, which played an important role in the formation of modern Brazilian national identity. This narrative was informed by his time spent accompanying the army as a reporter

---

1. 'Martha' in no. 22 and 'O Imaginario' in no. 24. The former consists of diary entries and the latter is a story; the style is consistent with that of *Inferno Verde*.

2. The editorial of the first issue states the intentions of this school: 'We want FEELING FOR FEELING'S SAKE and TRUTH FOR TRUTH'S SAKE.'

during the War of Canudos, which took place between the Brazilian state and a reactionary, royalist millenarian cult in the Northeast based around the charismatic leader Antônio Conselheiro. Although he was a staunch republican, da Cunha found himself unable to completely denounce the actions of the Conselheiristas. Greatly impressed by the bravery of the impoverished sertanejo population, his straightforward belief in Brazilian modernity was shattered by his feeling party to irrational state violence in the name of progress. He realised that metropolitan, coastal Brazil (which, despite the rise of Republicanism, was very much looking over its shoulder towards Europe) had neglected and failed to integrate various identities from the hinterland which could be considered more distinctively 'Brazilian'. The book is renowned for its highly detailed, scientific approach, blending reportage, essay, and expressionistic memoir—much like *Inferno Verde* itself. The latter should be read in this historical and political context, especially due to Rangel's own political trajectory from republicanism to monarchism.

Da Cunha had originally planned a book based around the Amazon in a similar style called *Um paraíso perdido* (*A Lost Paradise*) which was never completed. Some of the essays that would have been included in this projected work ended up in *À margem da história* (*On the Margins of History*). The similarities between the titles chosen by da Cunha and Rangel are interesting, partaking as they do—one Miltonic and one Dantesque—in a tradition of religious projection onto the Amazon extending as far back as the belief held by early explorers that it was the original site of the Garden of Eden. In *Inferno Verde*, the neobaroque appearance of a Gothic cathedral in the story 'A Good Man' brings this motif into sharp relief.

Verdant Inferno was written in Brazilian Portuguese and, even though Rangel grew up in Rio de Janeiro, it makes liberal use of a dialect which is specific to the Amazonas region. In this regard it is quite distinct from later works of Brazilian *modernismo* that take the Amazon as their setting, essentially produced by urban artists looking toward the interior. It is therefore full of language which is bound by history and geography, to the extent that it can be confusing even to native speakers of Brazilian Portuguese. To this end, L.G. de Simas published the *Elucidário*, a vocabulary and reference guide to *Verdant Inferno*.[3] Despite certain inaccuracies, as well as copious linguistic drift and taxonomic revisions, which we have updated, this has proved to be an essential reference. Many of the toponyms and names for flora and fauna have their etymology in Old Tupi. The most widely spoken form of Tupi during this period and in this region was Nheengatu, a descendant of Old Tupi which is still spoken today. This is historically tied to the notion of the *Língua Geral Amazônica*. When Jesuit missionaries arrived in Brazil, they codified what they found to be the most spoken language, that of the Tupinambá people. They compiled grammars after the fashion of Latin textbooks for distribution to other missionaries. The most famous example of this is Joseph of Anchieta's *Arte de gramática da lingoa mais usada na costa do Brasil* (1595). Padre Anchieta also wrote plays in Old Tupi, which number amongst the earliest classics of Brazilian literature. It was therefore used as a lingua franca for communicating with diverse Indigenous peoples across the Amazon, even if their own language was not part of the Tupi-Guaraní linguistic group. The legacy of this can be seen in 'The Eldest of the Mura', in which the Muran woman encountered by the narrator addresses the narrator in Nheengatu rather than a Muran language.[4]

Thomas Murphy

---

3. L.G. de Simas, *Elucidário do 'Inferno verde' de Alberto Rangel* (Genoa, 1908).

4. Pirahã, a Muran language that is still spoken today, has been the subject of major debate in linguistics in recent times. The linguist Daniel Everett has asserted that it is devoid of recursive structures, with the contention that this would serve as evidence against Noam Chomsky's theory of universal grammar. Various studies reporting the presence of varying degrees of embeddedness have emerged since.

Government plan from 1900 of an 'agricultural colony' at São José do Amatari. Alberto Rangel, 'Secretary of Lands, Mines, Navigation, and Colonisation', is credited as engineer on the project

Glossary

arreação A set of vertical strokes made by the rubber tapper to bleed the tree.

balance (carta de saldo) This term refers specifically to the document the rubber tapper receives or updates at the **barracão** when he purchases resources or settles his bills. This relationship was essentially a form of indentured servitude, since it was easy to amass a debt that would be mathematically impossible to pay off through the work of tapping. The journey upriver to the plantations was itself extremely costly.

barracão A building of central importance in Amazonian rubber plantations, generally combining various industrial, commercial, and domestic functions. The structure of these plantations was such that the barracão would be the hub, while the tappers themselves were stationed further afield, with their own assigned areas for rubber harvesting. The labourers would buy (more specifically, add to their **balance**) more supplies from this central building.

birdcage (gaiola) A type of steamer passenger vessel so-called because of the cage-like sides of the open decks, which often accommodated hammocks. These are still to be found on the Amazon River today.

brabos 'Braves': new recruits to the rubber plantations; novice **seringueiros**.

caatinga A type of semi-arid scrubland found in northeastern Brazil. *Caatinga* is a Tupi word meaning 'white forest/vegetation'. The term encompasses both distinctly arid regions (the **sertão**) as well as the more humid 'agreste' regions. Both are prone to sustained droughts, one of which is famously the initiatory event in Graciliano Ramos's masterpiece *Vidas secas*. Due to the background of a number of key characters, there is a subtle juxtaposition of Northeastern and Amazonian culture at play in *Verdant Inferno* and in Rangel's subsequent collection *Sombras n'agua*.

caboclo A person of mixed-race ancestry.

cabra Literally 'goat', this is slang for a daring or strong individual. The term also has racial associations and can mean 'mulatto' depending on the context.

campos geraes Vast open expanses of grassland with scattered shrubs and small trees found in the central and southern parts of Brazil.

canaranas A type of reed found frequently on the banks of the Amazon and its tributaries.

capoeira A term for the dense scrub that is prone to grow back after the land is burnt in slash-and-burn farming. When this occurs, it is extremely difficult to restore the land to a usable state, far more so than during the initial 'slashing' of the forest.

caucheros Rubber tappers, generally Peruvian, who felled Castilla trees to extract latex. The distinction between the Hispanic cauchero and the Brazilian **seringueiro** was seen as deeply significant by both da Cunha and Rangel. This can be seen in *Verdant Inferno* and in Euclides da Cunha's essay 'Os caucheros',[1] in which the author expresses earnest admiration for the exploratory spirit of the cauchero. The caucheros were roving nomads, while the seringueiros were sedentary and plantation-based. The cauchero method of tapping was more destructive, whereas the seringueiros would tap the same trees repeatedly.

Cearense Term for people from Ceará, a northeastern Brazilian state. Many **seringueiros** were originally from this region, which was hit by a series of terrible droughts at the end of the nineteenth century (most notably the 'Grande Seca'), leading to internal migration on an enormous scale.

coivaras Bundles of undergrowth remaining to be burnt after either the initial 'slashing' stage or the first burn in the type of slash-and-burn agriculture employed in the Amazon during this period. Northeastern immigrants were very familiar with these agricultural techniques as their use in that region goes back to the precolonial period.

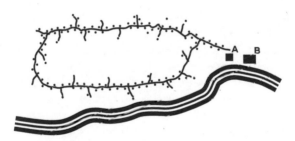

Schematic map of a **colocação**, showing the main circular **estrada** and secondary mangas. Black points indicate trees, **A** the **seringueiro**'s hut, **B** the **defumador**. After A. Chaves, *Exploração da Hevea no Territorio Federal do Acre, Rio de Janeiro* (1913)

colocação Literally 'placement' or 'position'. A patch of land for rubber harvesting, consisting of a circular **estrada** passing alongside numerous rubber trees, with small paths known as mangas branching off from it, along with a hut where the **seringueiro** dwelt, and a

---

1. Translated as 'The Caucheros' in da Cunha, *The Amazon*, 44–56.

defumador for smoking the extracted rubber. The life of the rubber tapper would be confined to this small area for months or years at a time, with infrequent trips back to the **barracão** to get their supplies and arrange their finances.

curumins A Nheengatu term for 'children' or 'kids'.

defumador Smoking hut used to smoke natural rubber.

estrada Normally 'road', this term however has a specific sense in the Amazon, referring to the narrow paths todden and retrodden by **seringueiros** in a **colocação**, allowing them access to the trees in the surrounding area.

fallen land (terra caída) Slang for the phenomenon whereby the intense hydrodynamic activity in the rainforest constantly erodes and reshapes the terrain.

furo Literally 'hole'. Streams, even smaller than tributaries or **igarapés**, which can be used to navigate laterally between lakes, rivers, and other channels by canoe. Both Euclides da Cunha and Alberto Rangel drew upon the Swiss-Brazilian botanist Jacques Huber's 1902 *Contribuição a Geographia Physica dos Furos de Breves*, which featured maps of these intricate networks. Great strides were being made in scientific potamology during the period, which da Cunha discusses with some excitement in the essay 'Rios em abandono'.[2]

heveas *Hevea brasiliensis*. Also known as the seringueira (hence **seringueiros**), the sharinga tree, or the rubber tree, this latex-producing plant in the Euphorbiaceae family was the driver of the Rubber Boom in Brazil.

Iara Also known as *Mãe das Águas*, or Mother of the Waters, a siren-like figure from Tupi-Guaraní mythology. They are said to have bodies

2. Translated as 'Rivers in Abandon' in da Cunha, *The Amazon*, 18–30.

MAPPA

dos Furos entre o Rio Amazonas e o Estuario do Pará

reduzido do "Mappa do Estado do Pará" do Engenheiro Henrique Santa Rosa, com algumas
modificações baseadas sobre os levantamentos de H. Coudreau (O. do Tajapurú)
e de J. Huber (Rio Aramá).

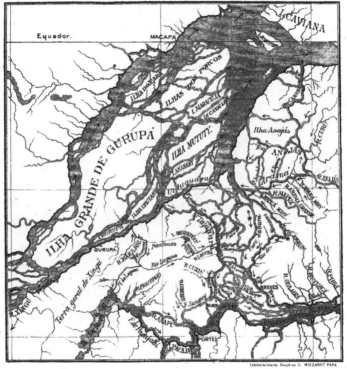

$$Escala = \frac{1}{2\,000\,000}$$

Map of the **furos** between the Amazon River and the Pará estuary, from
J. Huber, *Contribuição a Geographia Physica dos Furos de Breves* (1902)

that are part dolphin or fish, and a habit of luring passing men to a watery grave.

igapó A blackwater-flooded forest in the Amazon. These can sometimes be navigated by canoe. The term is from Old Tupi and means 'root forest'.

igarapé Small river or canoe path. From the Tupi: *igara*, canoe; *pé*: path, route.

jamaxis A type of pannier made of timbó (*Lonchocarpus nicou*) which **seringueiros** would use to carry their goods.

maloca A large communal dwelling, or long house, used by certain indigenous peoples in Brazil.

mocambo Also called quilombo, these were communities formed by escaped slaves in the forest. See Richard Price's *Maroon Societies: Rebel Slave Communities in the Americas* (Baltimore, MD: John Hopkins University Press, 1996) for a lengthy study on the subject.

montaria The same as 'mount' or 'steed' in English, this refers to a very specific boat—the most common type in *Verdant Inferno*. Its ironical name presumably derives from the indispensable nature of a boat of this size, or smaller, as a means of transport around the rainforest. **paxiúba** Euclides da Cunha called this the 'providential palm of the Amazon'. It provided the most commonly used wood for buildings and bridges in the region.

quicé From Old Tupi 'kysé':[3] a knife. Frequently used in the preparation of manioc.

---

3. E. de Almeida Navarro, *Dicionário de tupi antigo: a língua indígena clássica do Brasil* (São Paulo: Global, 2013), 248.

Engraving depicting a **montaria** to the far right, next to the larger galeota. It is possible to see the woven canopy mentioned a few times in Rangel's stories.

regatão Shop-boats that would travel around the Amazon river system selling goods (at a great profit) to those they encountered.

Engraving depicting a **regatão**.
From L.G. de Simas's *Elucidario do 'Inferno Verde' do Alberto Rangel*

A 1952 advertisement for Hotel Amazonas adopts Rangel's title, offering big game hunters deluxe suites with air conditioning right 'on the edge of the "Verdant Inferno"'

saudade A famously untranslatable Portuguese and Galician concept, which is also of major importance in Brazilian culture. It expresses, variously, nostalgia, melancholy, and longing, though it is paradoxically enjoyable and comforting. It is a common affective mode in Lusophone song writing. Saudade is mentioned in 'Catolé's Concept' in reference to Rosalia's dead husband as well as Malvina's present lover; the two women bond over a shared sensation mapped to quite distinct circumstances.

seringueiros Brazilian rubber tappers who worked on **Hevea** trees.

sertão The semi-arid backcountry found in the northeast of B[...]
The sertão has a mythic status in Brazilian literature: from Euclid[...]
da Cunha's groundbreaking *Os Sertões,* to figures such as João Gu[...]
marães Rosa, Ariano Suassuna and Maria Lucia Alvim. A detailed
study of literary representations of the sertão can be found in Antonio
Dimas's *Espaco e romance* (São Paolo: Editora Ática, 1987). The history of Brazilian literature, like that of other Latin American countries,
features a complex interplay between a tendency towards regional
expression—along with the attendant naturalism this requires—and
a passion for cosmopolitan experimentalism. This can clearly be seen
in the fusion of Parnassian, symbolist, and gothic tendencies with an
uncompromising attention to ethnographic, geographic, botanical,
and zoological detail in the work of Rangel. The Pernambucan writer
Osman Lins's notion of *ambientação* ('the set of known or possible
processes designed to instill the conception of a certain environment
in a narrative') captures this drive to forge a literary *Umwelt*.

sertanejo People from the **sertão**. Owing to the waves of immigra-
tion from Ceará prompted by drought and economic hardship, the
phrase recurs in *Verdant Inferno*.

tuxaua From Old Tupi *tuwi'xawa*: the a tribal chieftain. During the
period in which *Verdant Inferno* takes place, the term applied both
to leaders of more traditional social societies and to corrupt officials
who straddled both worlds, such as Colonel Roberto in 'Obstinacy'.

ubá A canoe: either a dugout from a single tree trunk or one constructed from bark. Also known as a canoa da casca (bark canoe) or
casco (dugout). Smaller and more versatile than the **montaria**.

várzea A whitewater-flooded forest in the Amazon.

SWITCH